Dream Weaver

By

Jamel P. Bates

In loving memory of R.W.P

ISBN 979-8-218-63371-4

Cover design by Helen Polsi
Edited by Jami Murphy

Acknowledgments

Thank you to all my friends and family for joining me on this journey. A special thanks to Drew and Meghan Dodson, Derick and Toni Graves, Angel and Kasie Esponiza, Colten, Randi and John Cooper, David and Lyla Green, my siblings, my children.

Most of all, thank you, Sam, for pushing me. It was you for a reason. Thank you so much.

Prologue

Before our story began, hundreds of years ago, in the Galaxy of Ryell, the first Emperor, Drew Cascade, craved more power and resources, so he announced to his people that his empire of Izeal would grow beyond their current world and conquer the known galaxy. At this time, Izeal's cities were forced to relocate to the sky due to pollution that made the surface unlivable after the War of Kings. The emperor ordered his best engineers and scientists to build giant industrial fans under the cities and fans on the planet's surface to hold the cities up in the sky. The Izealins, being both a brilliant and technologically advanced race, held these capabilities and more. Once his people were safe, the emperor set forth an order to start building space stations to travel the stars and conquer the other six planets in their galaxy; Ma'de, Rydean, Lanard, Tearocon, Newwart, and Osiris. Tearocon was the first planet he invaded for its rich and fertile lands, which he used to feed the campaign. Since the other civilizations were nomadic compared to the Izealins, with primitive weapons against advanced war machinery, the empire grew more powerful and unmatched by the other planets. Emperor Cascade expanded his empire by using the resources and people from his conquered worlds to increase his forces and wealth. Now, the Empire is ruled by Noah Cascade, the Fourth, and the Izealin Empire has continued to flourish under him. Despite the few rebellions over the years, it has remained steadfast. But now, with the galaxy on the brink of starvation, his people have begun to lose faith in him. Nothing was meant to last forever, right?

Chapter 1

The doorbell rings, and Roscoe rushes over to answer it, excited and nervous for the night. He stops by the mirror hanging on the wall to the right to ensure his curly black hair and clothes look suitable. He straightens up his tie and then runs his fingers through his hair. He focuses on the dimple on his right cheek, which stands out against his light brown skin, wondering to himself which of his parents he may have gotten it from. A tear wells up and rolls down from his eye as he brushes off the thought and wipes it away. "Not tonight." He shakes his head. "Tonight, will be a good night. I'm going to have a great birthday." He takes a deep breath to calm his nerves. "I got this." Roscoe opens the door.

Standing in the doorway is his best friend, Henry. He is taller than Roscoe, with dark brown skin and blonde dreads. Unbeknownst to Roscoe, he is accompanied by two women from Henry's apartment.

"Hello, Roscoe, what's up? Are you going to let us in or what? The beer is getting warm. Izeal to Roscoe." Henry weaves his hand in front of his face.

Roscoe stands there, confused. He thought it was just going to be the two of them tonight. He freezes for a second before replying. "Shoot, sorry, man. Come on in." Roscoe steps aside and gives Henry a look as he passes.

Henry, smirking, says, "Ladies, the birthday boy's name is Roscoe."

"Hi, I'm Tark," the short-haired brunette woman says.

Henry leans over. "I called dibs on that one."

Roscoe shakes his head at him.

The other woman walks around observing his place. "Hi, I'm Emily, I love your place, but it's missing one thing."

"What's that?" he replies as he walks into the living room, showing them to the couch.

She giggles, looking around at the bland, empty

room. "A woman's touch."

"Yeah, you think so. Is that what you do?"

"Yes, I'm an interior designer."

Roscoe looks around the room, which has a couch, TV, chair, and some old photos. He nervously chuckles. "Maybe you're right then. I'll have to look you up."

"It's interiors by Emily."

"Awesome, well, make yourselves at home. I'll play some music." He hurries and grabs the remote from the stand. "Hey Henry, can I speak with you in the kitchen for a second?" He turns on the music and then heads to the kitchen.

"Yeah, give me a second. Ladies, here are some beers. I need to talk to my boy." Henry smiles and opens the two beers for the girls before heading to the kitchen with the rest.

He enters the room, and Roscoe whispers, "What the heck, man? I thought it was just going to be the two of us?"

"Calm down, man. Have I not always had your back

since we were kids at St. Ethel's Boys Home?" Henry pats

Roscoe on the chest.

Roscoe bends over, rubbing his chest. "Yes, but," he

replies hesitantly, thinking of all the times Henry got him in

trouble over the years.

"You and Emily seem to be hitting it off, and I knew

if I didn't bring someone, you wouldn't talk to anyone at the

bar and end up the third wheel. I thought you'd be happy."

Henry walks over to the fridge and places the beers inside

then grabs two for them and shuts the door behind him.

Roscoe chuckles and shakes his head. "Henry, that's

not how that works, but thanks." He looks at her. "You are

right; she does seem nice."

"Good, let's just go have some fun tonight! I know

you don't drink but tonight for me." He hands Roscoe a

beer.

Roscoe shakes his head and grabs the beer. "Okay,

deal." They toast, pop the tab, and chug it. Then, they go

back into the living room with the girls. When they get in,

his cat Bean is sitting on Emily's lap getting attention.

She looks over at Roscoe. "He is so cute. What's his name?"

"Bean. Do you want me to get him down for you?" Roscoe replies, walking towards her.

"No, he's fine. He's such a good cat." Bean wraps his two tails around her arm, purring in delight.

He looks over at her beer. "Would you like another?"

She shakes it. "Yes, please."

Roscoe grabs a new beer for her before he sits back down.

"Thank you," she says while taking it, her yellow skin blushing red like her fire-red hair, a trait all Lanardians have.

"You're welcome," Roscoe says, feeling excited for the night. They drink and start playing games.

A half-hour later, Roscoe begins to feel an extreme cramping pain in his stomach. He runs to the bathroom and throws up.

Having followed him, Henry knocks on the door and

asks, "Are you ok, Roscoe?"

Curled up on the floor in pain, Roscoe replies, "No, I don't know what's happening, but I don't feel well. Just go ahead without me."

"Are you sure?" Henry asks, worried about him.

"Yeah, I'll catch up with you guys later." Roscoe holds his stomach as he stays curled up on the floor.

"Okay, we will be at Pokes Alley." He places his head on the door, concerned about leaving him. "Hey man, when you feel better, just get a speeder, and they will take you there. Remember -- Pokes Alley." Henry pulls away but casts a glance back at the bathroom door before leaving and heading out of the apartment with the girls.

Roscoe finds his footing and pushes himself up off the floor. He is sweating profusely, but he manages to stumble to his room. Once there, he removes his clothes and drops them on the floor as he staggers forward, still grasping at his stomach. He collapses on his bed and falls into a deep sleep.

"Dream a dream that will be lost in the deep, and forever, they shall weave!" A woman's voice says.

Roscoe awakes with a start, still sweating and out of breath, the woman's voice echoing in his head. Bean jumps up on the bed with him, startling him, pressing his paws down on his chest and meowing. Shaken by what happened, Roscoe takes a deep breath and sighs before getting up. "Come on, fat cat. Are you hungry?" He rubs his white and orange striped fur.

They walk to the kitchen, as he stumbles over empty beer cans and clothes from earlier. He gets to the kitchen and grabs a drink. Leaning up against the sink, he looks down at Bean. "What just happened to me, Bean?" Bean meows beside him, moving in and out of his legs. "Shoot my bad, buddy." He grabs a bowl from the top shelf and the milk jar from the near-empty refrigerator. He sets the bowl on the counter and fills it. Roscoe, still thirsty, grabs another glass of water. Then, he and Bean go outside onto the metal staircase of his skyline apartment and sit on the balcony overlooking the Capital city of Nines. The night seems fabulous, and the city is bustling as Roscoe places Bean's bowl of milk on the windowsill. A group of semis zoom by with the name Rex Tech on the side while Roscoe ponders the melodic voice he'd just heard. It continues to plague him over and over in his head.

"Dream a dream that will be lost in the deep, and forever, they shall weave!".

The voice is familiar, but Roscoe cannot quite grasp it. He thinks to himself, *who is she?*

Roscoe looks at his watch and sees that his shift starts in three hours. He returns to bed and lies back down, trying to sleep as he wrestles in and out of consciousness.

In his restlessness, Roscoe sees a womanly figure standing at the foot of his bed, with long, dark hair and a single blue streak running through it. "The Dream King is coming, and they will all serve him! Run before it is too late!" She urges before disappearing into a thick purple cloud of smoke.

Roscoe jumps up, scared and confused. He rubs his eyes, trying to figure out if he is awake. *Man, is this from the alcohol?* He thinks to himself, scratching his head. He glances over at his nightstand and his alarm clock reads 5:00 am. He jumps out of bed quickly because he must be at work by 6:00. Unsure of why his alarm did not go off, Roscoe goes to the bathroom and starts the shower before he walks to the living room and turns on the radio. Enjoying the music, he heads back to the bathroom and showers. As he gets ready for work, he pulls his uniform out of the closet: a light blue jumpsuit with a patch on the right side of his chest, reading Rex Tech. He pulls some food from the fridge for himself and some from the cabinet for Bean, placing it in his bowl on the hardwood floor. He grabs his thermos and lunch and heads to work. He presses his hand on the button on the wall, and the door shuts behind him.

A hooded figure walks to the edge of a mountainside

on Newwart and kneels in the snow, looking out at a valley of evergreen Bayhi trees before closing her eyes. When she opens them, she is in the Dream realm, and purple lighting strikes, showing the sizable black castle.

A voice bellows. "Did you feel that?"

"Yes, my king."

"Finally, we have found the boy. Bring him to me!" He smirks and turns his back.

"Yes, my king." she bows as she fades from the Dream realm. She stands up, returns to her ship, and flies off.

The Izeal Space Station 2625 was in orbit above Izeal. It resembled an anchor on its side, with the engines on the crown of the ship. The quarters, medical Bay, and other operations were in the shank. The station has cannons on the ship's bill.

Doctor Brooklyn Beal yells, "Captain on the bridge!"

Dr. Beal is an older woman who is close in age to the

captain. She has long, curly, dark brown hair with golden

brown tips and pieces of gray throughout. Her brownish-

green eyes hide behind her glasses, and just like all

Tearocons, she has a green diamond in the center of her

eyebrows, which stands out against her ivory skin.

Captain Ray Mitchell steps on the bridge, and

everyone stands up and salutes him. He is an older

gentleman from Izeal, tall and dark-skinned, with a crew cut,

mustache, and dark brown eyes. He is well-built for his age.

"As you were, " he orders in a deep voice that radiates

throughout the room. Everyone sits back down and

continues their work.

Dr. Beal approaches him. "Good morning, Captain."

Captain Mitchell walks up to the screen in the

bridge's center with a cup of coffee. "Good morning,

Doctor." He wipes his rank pin off on his traditional Izealin uniform. The uniform was all black with golden buttons down the center that read "IIS" for Izealin Imperial Soldier, matching the patch on the right side of their chest. The uniform is complete, with golden ruffles on the shoulder. Paired with black pants and black gravity-activating boots.

"So, how are things looking out there?" He asks as he takes a sip.

The soldier observes the radar screen and responds, "So far, all clear, Cap."

Captain Mitchell says, "Good. Keep an eye out on the outer planets. It has been the Wild West out there as of late. The Thug Lords are starting to get out of hand. We must keep the peace in these challenging times. It's our job."

A soldier comes running in with a message. "Captain," He urges out of breath.

"Calm down, soldier, " the captain says as the soldier catches his breath. "What is it?" he responds.

"We are hearing a lot of chatter in the comms room about the plant, Rex Tech, in the City of Nines might be bombed." He hands him the pad, showing him.

Dr. Beal tells Randi, the ship's A.I., concerned about the plant, "Bring up Izeal section 10." Randi brings it up, showing the production from the plant in question. "They are producing a lot of pills. Captain, we can't lose that plant. We are already starting to get low on pills from all the recent attacks."

"Are you sure it's *her?*" he asks.

"Yes, she is always there looking over things. I'm sure of it."

"Roger that, ma'am," he says. Captain Mitchell radios his team. "Load the Dark Wolf. We are going to capture her this time."

Roscoe walks out of his building and unlocks his

mini speeder. He climbs on and puts his stuff in his

basket. He grabs the handlebars, turns on the two-fan

hoverboard, and presses the start button on the control

panel.

The holograph between the handlebars appears.

"Where would you like me to take you, sir?"

"Work, please."

The speeder races down Nine's sidewalk to get

him to work. As it passes by St Ethel's boys' home, he

sees all the cars lined up for food. He shakes his head.

Man, is this what it has come to? Roscoe remembers that

few people went to the food drives as a child.

Nevertheless, he keeps going until he pulls up to

the front gate of Rex Tech and parks his speeder. He

walks up to the front door and goes in. He clocks in as

he walks through the plant. He sees Henry at their

station and walks up to him. "What's up, man? Are you

not cold?"

Henry is wearing a pair of goofy-looking goggles that his parents gave him before they died on a fishing trip. His jumpsuit is tied off at the hip, revealing his muscles through the white T-shirt underneath. "How are you feeling? Are you still unwell? You look drained. Did you not get any sleep last night after I left your place? Was it that bad?"

Roscoe responds., "Honestly, I don't know what happened last night. I couldn't sleep at all after those drinks. I kept hearing this woman's voice, but I…" He pauses.

"What is it? You are acting weird." Henry asked.

Roscoe leans in and whispers, "I could have sworn I was sleeping."

Henry looks around and replies, "I have heard about this before, but I have never heard of anyone doing it."

"What is it, Henry?" Roscoe is eager to know.

"I believe you did what the Elders once called DREAMING."

Roscoe steps back in shock. "Henry! That can't

be true. That has not happened since the old days.

What's going on? I'm scared, man."

"Don't worry, Roscoe. Everything will be okay."
Henry bends down and presses the button to start their
machine. "So, what was it like?" Henry says, pondering
on what Roscoe told him.

At that moment, Roscoe looks up and sees three
people in hooded purple robes talking to his manager before
he points at him. Roscoe gets a weird feeling, and he turns
to Henry. "Something is wrong, man. We've gotta get out of
here."

Henry is confused. "What do you mean?"

Feeling very off about the situation, Roscoe shouts
to Henry, "Just trust me, man. Let's go!" He points towards
the exit.

"Okay!" Henry replies as they start running to the
back of the plant.

Just as they reach the back door, Captain Mitchell

enters, and a rough-looking older man follows. The man is pale-skinned, dark-brown-eyed, with a bald head and a long braided black ponytail down his back. He has a scar going straight down the left side of his face, starting from the top of his head and ending just below his cheekbones, and a blue arrow across the bridge of his nose, like other native people of Osiris.

He and Cap lock eyes with the hooded figures chasing Roscoe.

Captain Mitchell yells, "Get down!" Henry and Roscoe drop to the floor as they pull their blasters out and aim them at the hooded figures.

Suddenly, fire erupts from both sides, and orange colors fill the room in the blink of an eye. Workers run and scream in a panic. During the chaos, one of the workers gets wounded in the crossfire. The room echoes with the sounds of war, explosions, and blaster rounds hitting the machines. Cap shoots a hooded figure in the head as Razor pulls out his hatchet and throws it. It slices through the air and buries itself in one of the attacker's heads. Silence

follows.

The pair find Roscoe and Henry hiding under a machine.

Captain Mitchell reaches down to grab Roscoe's

hand, and says, "Come on, kid. We got you."

Henry gets up first, wiping himself off. Just as

two female soldiers walk in from the front of the plant,

he says, "Don't worry; I got it."

Captain Mitchell helps Roscoe to his feet. "Are

you ok?"

"Yeah, I think so. Thank you." He wipes himself

off.

"No problem, kid."

Two women approach the group. They both look

to be in their mid-20s. One of the women says, "Hey,

cap it's all clear over here." She is a tall, stern-faced

woman with short black hair, fair skin, and blue-gray

eyes like the women of Newwart. The other woman

behind her has blonde braided hair, and brown, umber

skin like the natives of Ma'de. Her eyes are as blue as Ma'de's waters. She is much shorter in stature than the first.

"Roger that," Cap replies.

The group walks up to the last hooded figure lying on the ground, moaning in pain from her wounds from the firefight.

"Where is she, and why were you after these boys?" Captain Mitchell bends down, hovering over her.

She says nothing but spits in Captain Mitchell's face.

In a moment, Razor draws his katana from its sheath and puts it to her throat.

Cap wipes his face off and says, "I will only ask you one more time. Where is she, and what do you want with these boys?"

She yells, "I will say nothing. Long live The Dream King!" Before clenching down her jaw. Seconds later, purple smoke oozes between her lips, and she begins to convulse.

Henry freaks out and jumps back. "What the hell is that?"

Roscoe remembers what the woman said last night. He drops to his knees, grabs her, and shakes her. "Why did you say that?"

He gets no response as her convulsions become worse. Captain Mitchell pulls him back when he realizes the woman hid a cyanide pill in her teeth. "Fuck! Lily, hurry!"

Lily grabs her medical bag to save her, but it is far too late.

Captain Mitchell turns to Roscoe and says, "Why were you worried about what she said? Have you heard it before, boy? Tell me your names, now."

"No, sir. I have no idea. My name is Roscoe, and this is my best friend, Henry," he replies shakily.

"I am Captain Ray Mitchell, and this is my second in command, Razor," he points at the older man. This is my weapon specialist, Ophelia." The stern-faced woman

nods. And my pilot, Lily Prices." She waves at Roscoe.

"So, guys, listen. We need to know why they were after

you."

"We don't know anything, sir, nor do we know

who they are."

"Seems like it to me you've heard that saying

before."

"No, sir. As I said, I have no idea who they are or

what she was talking about. I'm just as lost as you guys

are," he replies, not telling him the whole truth because

he is unsure who to trust.

"We will find out, so just tell us the truth." Razor

orders.

He becomes very nervous and replies, "I'm telling

you the truth, sir. I don't know."

"Very well, then. We will find out." He turns back

to his team. "Everyone up!" Cap says to his team.

Ensuring the room was secure.

They all respond, "Up cap."

He radios the Izeal Federation Station 2625. "We're all clear down here. We are going to need medics. We've got injured civilians. Dark Wolf over and out."

A woman's voice over the radio replies, "Is the plant good, Cap?"

"Yes, there is a little damage, but still operational. I don't think they were here to destroy the plant though."

"What do you mean?" she presses.

"I have two civilians in custody. I believe they were going after the civilians, not the plant."

"Bring them to the station and we will figure it out, Cap," she answers.

"Okay. Over and out," he responds. He turns to his team. "You heard the doctor. These two are coming with us. The medics and local soldiers can handle the rest. Load up!"

Roscoe hesitates to go with them, thinking back on all the times imperial soldiers would take people, and they would not return. "Wait, Sir, thank you for your help, but we must get home."

Captain Mitchell says, "Come on, boys, I don't think that is the best decision. We can protect you, I promise."

Roscoe looks at Henry, then back at Cap, and says, "I don't know, sir. No disrespect, but I have heard that before."

Henry, perplexed by the whole situation, whispers to Roscoe "Man, what is going on?"

Roscoe, who is just as confused as Henry, replies "I don't know, man, shit."

Captain Mitchell interrupts them. "Listen, fellas. We are the good guys. All we want to do is get to the bottom of this, and then you can go home."

Scared but trying to put on a brave face, Henry says, "How do we know that?"

Razor gets a little irritated, saying, "Well, it seems that you guys need to look around. If we wanted to hurt you, we would have."

Roscoe looks around and is still hesitant to go.

Cap raises his voice. "Look fellas, we both want answers, right?"

"Yes, we do, sir," Roscoe nervously answers.

Cap softens his voice. "Okay then, let's figure this out together, and we can protect you if more of them." He points at the hood figures.

Roscoe looks around the room and then at Henry, who shakes his head. "Okay, then. I'll come with you," he says.

Henry grabs his arm. "Are you sure about this?"

Roscoe nods and answers, "Look around. They are right, what other options do we have? If they can find us here, they can find us anywhere. We are safer with them."

Henry shakes his head, not liking the plan, and

replies, "OK, fine. Then I hope you are right." Henry

sighs. I'm coming with you."

"Henry, you don't have to come." Roscoe pleads

with him.

"Come on man. You know I go where you go."

They clasp each other in a brief hug. "Thanks,

brother. I love you."

"Brothers for life," Henry replies as they release

each other.

"Okay, let's go. This way then," Cap says. They

head back to the exit, and he radios Dr. Beal back. "We

are on our way; we will be there shortly."

"Roger that, see you in a few," Dr. Beal states.

They led Roscoe and Henry out the back door

and onto a hangar, where a massive metal ship that

looked like a sloop ship was waiting. It had a Black

Wolf's face on the side of it and one with its mouth

open on the ship's bow. It had multiple modifications

that allowed it to go into deep space. It was just there,

hovering over the landing pad. Roscoe and Henry looked up at the massive ship in amazement.

Captain Mitchell sees their reactions and says, "I know I did the same thing the first time I saw it."

Lily turns her wrist and radios Randi, the Dark Wolf computer. "You can lower the ladder now, Randi. Thank you." A rope ladder comes down, and the crew begins to climb.

Henry goes up first, and then Roscoe climbs up behind him. He lands on the deck. Henry grows excited when he sees the cannon blaster guns on either side. He runs behind one and pretends to shoot.

Watching him, Razor says, "They can be fired automatically or manually."

"Wow, just like the games." Henry loves playing war video games, so this is his dream come true.

Lily giggles. "Your friend is something else."

Roscoe smirks. "He can be."

Captain Mitchell jumps on the deck and says, "Ok,

that's enough. Everyone inside so we can take off."

"Dang it, maybe some other time," Henry says as he runs over to catch up with the group.

As they walk inside the Dark Wolf, Roscoe, being his usual self, becomes anxious. Walking down the hall, he says, "I have questions."

Henry interrupts him. "Yeah, what were you guys doing at our plant anyways?"

A dwarf walks up behind them with a pipe in his mouth. Loading his tobacco, he answers, "Within due time, big boy." Jeff is a dwarf and a native Rydeanin. His freckles and orange curly hair match his beard, which pops out on his pasty white skin. He is stocky, even for a dwarf.

Lily enters the bridge behind him and says, "We must take off now. We can finish this at the Station." She takes her seat in the pilot's chair. "Okay, Randi, turn off the autopilot. I'll take it from here."

Randi replies, "OK, Lily, right away."

Lily takes control of the ship. "Everybody buckle up." They all take their seats except for Razor, who shows Roscoe and Henry how to buckle up.

Razor stands over Henry and points at his armrest. "You see that button on your right there? That button will make your buckle come out over both shoulders."

Henry does it and it pulls him up close to the chair. "Dang this is tight."

"You want it that way. We go fast on take-offs." Razor explains.

Roscoe presses the button and his buckle comes down. Excited, he says, "Lily, was that what I think it was?"

"Yes," she responds, giggling at his excitement. "It is the robotic autonomous network diagnostic intelligence. We call her Randi. Okay everyone, strap up. We're heading to the station." The ship's sails open, and a silver metallic vinyl fabric drops. The sails provide a shield that protects the vessel and helps it navigate the waters and stars.

As they are about to take off, Roscoe remembers Bean and yells, 'Wait, Bean!"

They all look at him confused. "Who or what is a Bean?" Jeff asks.

"My cat," he responds.

They all shake their heads and laugh.

Razor buckles himself in, and says, "You want us to wait on a cat."

Roscoe says, "No, I can call my old nosy neighbor, Miss Clark. She can watch and feed Bean while I'm gone." He turns his wrist over, and his watch shows a hologram of Miss Clark's apartment number, 1317. He calls and it continues to ring. No answer. "I'll leave a message. Miss Clark, can you watch and feed Bean for me? I'll be off world for a while and don't know when I'll return. Thank you." Roscoe hangs up.

Razor sarcastically says, "Are you ready now?" as he looks sternly at Roscoe.

Roscoe stutters and says, "Y-yes, sir."

"Don't call me sir. That's only for the captain." Razor snapped back.

Captain Mitchell says, "Easy now, Razor."

Razor replies, "Yes, sir!"

"Razor has always been a bit edgy with new people, but you get to know him, and he is softer than a Silver tail." Captain Mitchell says to Roscoe with a chuckle. The engines fire up, and they head into outer space.

Lily radios Federation Station 2625 as they draw near. "This is the Dark Wolf ready for docking."

The station pilot responds, "All clear for docking. Welcome home, sister."

She gets excited and says, "See you soon, big brother."

Roscoe looks out the window of the Dark Wolf,

seeing space for the first time, and is in utter awe of it.

As they approach the Izeal Federation Station, the drop ship pulls into the loading hanger. When it lands, everyone starts to exit and go their own way, but Captain Mitchell tells Roscoe and Henry,

"This way," Cap tells them. He then leads them down the hallway to the bridge, where a woman with long dark brown hair and glasses, who looked about mid 40s, and a tall, thin man with a curly blonde Fro-hawk are waiting.

The man looks up, and glances at Roscoe and Henry before looking back at the holographic monitor in the center of the room.

They walk up to the woman and Roscoe says, "Ma'am, were you the one on the radio?"

"Yes, I am Dr. Beal. Welcome to The Federation Station 2625."

More soldiers enter the bridge, and Roscoe starts to feel anxious with them around him. "Can you please tell me what the heck is happening and who those people were?"

"Yes, but first I need you to tell me why they wanted you guys."

"Like I told the captain earlier, I don't know."

"Well, those people that were after you and your friend are followers of a ghost. We call them his acolyte."

Roscoe said, "Well, with all due respect, ma'am, they don't think he is dead."

She said, "I know he is."

"How do you know?" he responds.

She yells, "Because I was there!" Turning her back to everyone. She pauses, turns back, and says, "Twenty-two years ago, a group of scientists figured out the Sun was dying, and we would eventually no longer be able to grow crops, that you already know. What you don't know is that the emperor held a private meeting with all of them. One of them, a renowned scientist from Newwart named Darren Aspen, said he had an

idea for fixing the sun. He said there were other realms,

and we must go to the Dream Realm to save the Sun

and humanity. People thought he was crazy for even

thinking he could enter that plane of consciousness

without sleeping. They laughed him out of the room,

and he got angry and stormed out of the conference,

vowing he would. So, he searched the planets for the

materials he needed to build and stabilize a portal, trying

to prove them wrong. One day, he said he had

everything he needed to build and keep it stable, but he

never told us how he knew what materials to get. It took

him a few weeks to build it, and when finished, he called

us to his lab on Mt. Tocan. When we got there, he had

already built the portal. We tried a test run and sent

some things through to ensure it was safe for travel.

Everything seemed safe, so Emperor Noah ordered us

to go through the portal. We were on this huge land

mass with giant plants and flowers as tall as men when

we stepped through. They were different shades of orange, red, and blue. It was the most peaceful place I had ever encountered. It made me feel full of joy, warmth, and comfort. I had this overwhelming feeling that no matter what, I could do anything. We made our way through and eventually got to the cliff's edge and looked over. All we could see was a neon blue water-sand-like substance all around, as far as the eye could see. It was a tremendous drop to the bottom, so we started testing everything around us and returning it to our labs on the other side of the portal. Sadly, nothing seemed to work. So, one day, Dr. Aspen and a group set off to the lowest point on the cliff's side. They lowered someone down until he reached the bottom. He radioed up that he had retrieved the samples, but as he was coming back up, the line started to come apart. It made him jerk, and the samples started falling out of his backpack. He caught the last one just as it was falling out. We hurried and tried to get him up, but the rope broke when he reached the top of the cliff. Dr. Aspen

reached out and caught his hand. He yelled, "I got you,

don't let go!" He told the doctor to take the sample.

Just as he handed the sample to Dr. Aspen, the guy lost

his grip and fell. We searched for him for hours up and

down the cliffside but found nothing. We decided to

hurry and get the last sample to the lab to ensure it was

safe. Due to what happened, we made it off-limits to be

by the cliff's edge. We would find another way. Dr.

Aspen was so depressed over the young man's death

that he started spending more time in the Dream realm,

mainly by the cliffs, looking for a sign of him. The loss

of the man and the pressure of trying to save everyone

drove the doctor mad. I believe these things started to

change, Doctor Aspen. We noticed he was changing

physically and mentally. He did not need his glasses and

no longer favored his right leg; he'd hurt as a young man

in a Reaver attack. He started telling us about our

dreams that no one else knew about. He was making no

sense, often talking gibberish about crystals, some Mirror, and a shadowy figure. We thought he was going mad, but what he said next concerned us greatly. He said, why do we need to save everyone? We can start over with just the elite like us with no more Izealin rule. That was not the man who was my mentor. He was a kind and loving man, not this. It was as if he and the Dream Realm were becoming one. What once felt warm and inviting was now cold and made you shiver in fear. The plant life was starting to fade away as well. This dark purple nebula replaced the warm light that lit this once beautiful place. Dr. Aspen looked like a younger man again, built and fit. We asked him what was happening to him, and he said, "I have found the truth, and so we will begin the purification. It will all be mine." After he said this, the ground began to rumble, and a huge black stone castle appeared. He looked at us and said, "I control the Dream realm now! I alone have the power to save us."

I had said, "No, you mean to rule us. You're a madman!"

He replied, "Join me or die!"

We yelled, "Never!"

So my best friend and I ran for the entrance to the portal. On our way, some soldiers stopped and fired back at him to buy us time. He brought up this purple smoke, which grabbed them and slammed them to the ground, knocking them out. We got to the entrance and set the charges to blow the portal so he could not escape to the living realm. We were about to finish placing the charges on the portal when the man he slammed to the ground just moments ago rose and was now under his control. They started shooting at us. We had no other choice but to blow it and trap them there. The emperor did not want any of this to get out and start a rebellion, so we were sworn to secrecy."

Roscoe says, "So what happened to the sample you

brought back?"

She paces the bridge. "The watery sand-like

substance we named it Pearium. It is pure divinity. Like

you and me, it contains life and death particles, which are

also in all living things. I believe this could heal the Sun,

but the amount we had was not enough. Out of fear of

letting the Doctor out of the Dream Realm, returning to

get more was not an option. But what we didn't know was,

he had already escaped. We didn't know what he could do,

and when we realized it, we were too late. He had already

taken four of the most renowned scientists, brainwashed

them and made them bomb our food warehouses and

storage soon after. He was looking for something, but we

couldn't figure out what. Three of them are dead now, and

the other one is my best friend," Dr. Beal pauses

"so what did he do to them?!"

We call it "Dream Weaving." As far as we can tell,

he manipulates people in their dreams."

Roscoe, confused, "So we all used to dream?"

She replies, "yes, The EnergyP pill. I created it to keep everyone from dreaming. The emperor had me lie to everyone and say it was for nutrients for the lack of food."

He looks down, thinking, "*Then why am I dreaming again? Could it have been the alcohol?*" He looks up again and says to her, "So what does all that have to do with us?"

She says, "I don't know, but they clearly wanted one of you. So, we will find out together what they want, I promise." She puts her hand on Roscoe's shoulder.

He says, "Okay, Thank you, what now, then?"

She says, "We gotta get out of here. She will be here soon. She is never too far behind."

Roscoe replies, "Who is she? Do you know her?" He is very curious about her.

"She is just someone who has lost their way," she says before quickly changing the subject. "Cap, while you guys were on your way up, I spoke to the emperor about what happened at the plant, and he ordered us to find the items Dr. Aspen used to build the portal and build our own." She closes her journal.

Roscoe is confused. "You just said he was bad. Why are we going to him now?"

She sighs. "You know that sample I had?"

"Yeah."

"We are almost out, and once it's all gone, no more pills, he can get what he is looking for. Also, the Sun does not have much time left."

"Well, I guess I'm in." He says hesitantly.

"Good. Very well then. This mission is top secret, so we won't get back up." She turns her attention to the window and looks out at Izeal. "Randi set a course for Fiafia."

Woah. We are going to one of Ma'de's moons? *This is wild.* Roscoe thinks to himself, overjoyed to get to see it up close.

She turns back to the group. "We can plan there before

heading down to San-Van to collect the Windomm we

need."

Randi responds, "Yes, doctor."

Dr. Beal looks at Roscoe and Henry and says, "You

two have had a long day. Get showered and get some

food. Also, go to the medical bay and get your pills

refilled. Everyone keeps their containers on them." She

shows them a rectangular metal box with these clear

hexagon-shaped pills in it. "Luke?"

"Yes Dr. Beal." He stands up from the monitor.

"Will you show them to their rooms?"

"Yes Dr. Beal. Follow me guys."

"Roscoe, hopefully, we can get a chance to talk

more later."

"Sure thing, thank you," Roscoe says as Henry and

he follow Luke off the ship's bridge. As they walk out,

Henry leans over to Roscoe and whispers, "So what are

you going to do about the dreaming?"

Roscoe shrugs and says, "I don't know yet, but I'll

figure something out."

"You better. That place sounds scary."

Before Captain Mitchell leaves the bridge, he notices a weird and complex look on Dr. Beal's face. He walks up to her. "What's up, Doc?"

She nods and walks over to the corner of the room, which he follows. "I know who that little one is; I think that's who they are after."

Captain Mitchell with a puzzled look reply, "You do. Who is he?"

She lowers her head and whispers, "He is her son."

He gets loud, "What?! He is Rachel's son?"

She shushes him. "Yes, quiet." She leans closer. "I cannot forget those dimples. He looks just like she did when she was younger. I only saw him one time, and that was years ago." She shakes her head. "I lost track of him after I dropped him off after Rachel

disappeared."

He asks her, "Do we tell him the truth about his

mom?"

She thinks briefly and replies, "No, we should

keep this between us. We have too many questions and

not enough answers."

"What puzzles me is why they are after him now.

After all these years, what changed?" Cap replies,

rubbing his goatee

"I don't know but they want Roscoe for

something, and we have no clue what that is. So, I think

the best plan is to keep him close and in the dark for

now."

He says, "Okay, I'll go with it, but I don't like

this plan. Being upfront with him would go a long way

toward keeping him on our side."

She says, "We are three days away from Ma'de.

Get some food and rest, and when we get close, we will discuss what to do next, Cap."

"You got it, Doc," as he heads off the bridge.

Chapter 2

The Dream King's general kneels on the floor of her drop-ship and closes her eyes. As she opens them, the air around her begins to shift. Purple lightning cracks and the castle's silhouette appears. As she walks to the castle, purple smoke billows around her feet. She enters the black door and makes her way to the throne room.

The Dream King enters his throne room with his violet robes tied loose around his waist, sweeping across the black marble floor, disturbing the purple smoke around his feet. Standing at the foot of the stairs, the general watches silently under her purple hood as he storms past her up the stairs to his throne. His intense and commanding gaze swept the room, his amethyst crown gleaming between the horns protruding from his head. He turns around, and a mass of purple smoke materializes into a throne, which he settles upon. The throne was adorned with intricate patterns and shimmered with a faint luminescence. It seemed to bend to his will, solidifying its presence as he made himself comfortable.

The general looks around the room at his Summation knights who entered behind The Dream King. They all surround the throne room in unison, resting the handles of their double-bladed axes on the cold stone floor next to them. The Dream Realm changed them so much that they are more like beasts than the men they once were. Now, they have matted hair growing over their face. Their eyes are as Red as the moon of Rydean, and their teeth are sharp as razors. Their armor is the same deep purple as The Dream King's crown.

"What happened to the boy?" The Dream King roared. Rachel's eyes quickly came back to his, now complete with anger.

Rachel lowers her hood and kneels. "My king, I'm sorry I have failed you. They got him."

He leans forward. "How could you let this happen?" He slams his hand down on his throne. "You know what he means to me!"

She lowers her head in shame. "I know, my king, but they know nothing. We will get him back, I promise," she pleads.

His expression softens. "Dear niece, did I not save you and give you the power you needed to get your revenge against the ones who have wronged you?"

"Yes, my king, you know I am grateful and loyal to you and only you."

"Then do what I need done or I will send someone else."

"No, I can handle it. He is no one to me. If I had to, I would end his life for you. Long live The Dream King!" she chants.

He rises and steps down the stairs, stopping right above Rachel. He leans down and touches her face, lifting her chin to look into her eyes. "Well then, since they have no idea what I need him for, go get him before they can figure it out!" He lets go of her chin and returns to his throne. "Oh, and niece, don't fail me again!" He growls, looking over his shoulder at her, before retaking his place on his throne.

She places her hood atop her head. "Yes, my king." Then, she disappears into a cloud of purple smoke.

Back on the Federation Station, Roscoe is sitting on a bench, looking out into the abyss and wondering what his role is in all of this. He starts to nod off, and when he opens his eyes, he is in the Dream Realm. He looks around in fear. Purple lightning strikes, and he sees The Dream King's castle. He begins to shake all over, realizing where he is.

He hears The Dream King's voice saying, "This way to the truth you seek, boy." He steps closer to the castle before suddenly being shaken awake.

Standing over him was Lily. "Hey, I'm sorry to wake you, but we are here." The station was flying on the dark side of Fiafia, Ma'de's moon. Her eyes were big and bold, and she was excited to be home. "It's been a while since Luke, and I have seen our family." She looked down at him and noticed he seemed elsewhere and afraid. "Are you doing, okay?"

He starts to tell her what he saw but stops. He doesn't know if he can trust her yet. "I'm okay. I'm just tired." He rubs his eyes and stretches. "Okay, I'm ready; let's go."

She brushes it off. "Okay, then. Everyone else should be heading to the hangar bay by now." They walk down the hallway to the hangar.

As Lily and Roscoe make their way to the hangar, Roscoe thinks to himself. *What is that voice talking about? What is the truth and how am I able to get there?"*

Captain Mitchell is leaning up against a crate, waiting for them as they walk in. "Good. Everyone is here. Now, we are here to resupply and get the

Windomm. We need it to build a portal to the Dream Realm. Roscoe, you will come with us. I want you to always stay with someone. We have enemies everywhere. You understand?" He looked at Roscoe with a stern face, waiting for his reply.

Roscoe feels slightly peeved for being treated like a helpless child. "Yes, sir, but I can help you know."

Captain Mitchell checks his gear. "You are helping by always staying safe and staying with one of my guys." He looks at everyone else and says, "You all understand, at all times?"

Everyone replies, "Yes, sir!"

Henry, feeling left out, says, "What about me? I'm sorry, but where he goes, I go sir."

"Henry, look, we don't want to leave Dr. Beal by herself. Your job is to protect her."

"He and I need to stay together. Right, Roscoe?" Henry waits for his answer.

Roscoe walks over to him and says, "Listen, I'll go with them and try to find out more about what's happening. You stay with the doctor and learn what you can from her."

"I will." Henry grabs the back of Roscoe's neck and puts their foreheads together. "Be safe out there, my brother."

Roscoe replies "I will." He walks back over and grabs his bag.

"Okay Cap, I'll stay back to help protect the Doctor." Henry leaves the hangar bay.

"Hey Cap. Do we have time to stop by our parents' house? It's been a while since we have seen them." Luke asks.

"We have a few hours, so you guys should be okay. Chancellor Riley asks to see me as well. So, you are good to see your family, and we will meet later in the market," Cap said.

"Yes, sir!" Luke and Lily both replied.

"Oh, and if your mom is at the Command Center, I'll tell her you are home."

"We are Entering Ma'de's orbit," Randi says over the intercom.

"Okay, let's load up the Dark Wolf," Captain Mitchell says.

The team gets on the Dark Wolf and flies out of the Station.

As the ship lowers into Ma'de's atmosphere, Lily lands it on the water and says, "Randi, open up the sails."

"Yes, Lily," she responds, and the sails open. They begin to journey into the port of San-Van, one of the biggest cities on Ma'de.

Roscoe walks out on the deck of the Dark Wolf and hangs over the ledge, letting the water splash his hand. He looks at the two-story brick buildings in awe of all the drop-

ships in the port. They pull up to a ramp and lower the
anchor.

They join him on the deck, and Captain Mitchell
says, "Let's get what we came for. Remember, our mission
is top secret. No one can know the real reason why we are
here. Keep your eyes peeled as well."

"Yes, sir!" they all say as they walk down the ramp.

The crew makes their way up the dock through the
crowd, and Roscoe looks at all the drop-ships with
different insignia but sees no city. "So, how do we get to
the city?"

Captain Mitchell passes him. "Come on, you will see.
Keep up. Luke, go check the ship in."

They walk into the Check-in station. "You got it,
Cap."

Luke walks over to the man behind the glass. "Hey,
Chief, how are you doing?" Luke asked the Chief as he
leaned on the windowsill.

"It's a beautiful day, can't complain."

"Good. Well, I'm checking in The Dark Wolf," Luke says through the radio.

"Does it need any maintenance?" The chief asks.

"No, we should be good. We are just here for some Windomm from the market and supplies."

"Very well, you are checked in. Good day."

"You as well, " Luke replies, walking away to join the others. They then enter the elevator, which lowers them beneath the water and into the glass city of San-van.

Roscoe looks out of the glass elevator at the incredible city. He is amazed by its beauty, seeing it for the first time. The city goes for miles, with glass buildings and other structures made of windomm that glistens off the glass, making the whole place shine with magnificent beauty. They built their houses, roads, and sidewalks out of windomm.

Roscoe looks back at Lily and Luke. "Wow! How many people live here?"

Lily looks at him and laughs. "At least five hundred

and fifty thousand, I believe, give or take."

Roscoe looks back at her, shocked by the sheer number of people. "Are you kidding me? I have never seen that many people in one place. There are more people here than on Nines."

They reach the city and exit the elevator. Captain Mitchell says, "Razor and I will go to the Command Center to check on things here and see if the fish is ready for the food transport. Lily and Luke, you go home, see your parents, and see how they are doing. Ophelia and Jeff, you take the kid to the city market and get the windomm we need for the portal and other supplies."

Still hungover from the night before and head pounding, Jeff responds, "Cap, come on now. Why do we get stuck with the kid?"

"Shut up, Jeff," Ophelia slaps him upside the head. "If you didn't drink all night, you would not be hurting right now." She turns back to Captain Mitchell. "Yes, sir. We are on it, Cap."

"Fine." Jeff rubs his head as he follows them. "By the way, O, that hurt, Hungover, remember? Dang!"

"I did." She smirks while walking off and leading Roscoe down an alley into the market. Roscoe looks down the road, left and right, and there is nothing but shop after shop on either side. The elevator door opens next to him, and people step off and walk toward the market.

"Where are they all coming from?" Roscoe asks.

"Glass tube elevators run from city to city throughout Ma'de," Ophelia answers, pointing at the tubes.

Roscoe looked out the glass. "We have something like that on Nines, but it's off-limits. Only the workers are allowed to use them."

"If you don't know how to use these, you can get lost and end up in any of Ma'de's cities." She shows him a map of the tunnels and how they cross and intertwine. Roscoe looks at the map over. "Well, come on, let's keep moving. We must get the windomm."

They make their way down the street, and Roscoe

looks around at the different colors of silks made from the bare skin seahorses' silk web they weave. These silks hang on lines that run over the tops of each market building.

Roscoe covers his nose as they make their way down the road. "Man, what is that smell?"

Mmm. Jeff breathes in deep. "That's this morning's haul. You can purchase all types of fish on the ground level and other sea life, like Pearl Squid, which was once a tremendous delicacy in these parts. Now, they are found in fewer and fewer shops. It's such a shame." Jeff shakes his head.

Ophelia points at some stairs. "That's where we need to go. Come on, this way." Roscoe follows her as Jeff brings up the rear. "All shops related to windomm work, food banks, and other supply shops should be on the second level."

As Roscoe walks behind Ophelia, he briefly recognizes an apparition of the woman he saw in his dream before she disappears again. He hears a whisper through the crowd: "Roscoe."

He looks around, but no one is there. He keeps walking. One minute, she is there; the next, she is gone. She appears in and out of sight throughout the market as they make their way up the stairs. Walking into the Windomm shop, he hears it again. "Roscoe." And she disappears.

He glances over his shoulder and sees nothing again. Ophelia looks back at him and says, "Hey, are you coming?"

Startled, Roscoe replies, "Yes, sorry." He looks back one last time to see if she is there and sees nothing, so he enters with them.

Still angry about having to watch after Roscoe and having a hangover, Jeff marches through the busy shop, up to the merchant, agitated, and says, "Hey buddy, can we get two sheets of windomm?"

The merchant, an older man, leans over the

counter. "That sure is a lot. What are you building, if you don't mind me asking, little guy?"

Jeff pulls out his Hammer blaster and aims it at the merchant. His smirk quickly faded and was replaced with fear. He throws his hands up.

Jeff, pissed off now, shoves the barrel of his blaster right up his nose. "Do not insult me. I am not a child, and that's a lot of questions, young man. Who are you working for?"

The merchant trembled with his hands still raised in the air.

"Nothing to say about my height now, huh?"

"No. I mean no disrespect, sir, I forgot my glasses."

Ophelia shakes her head at Jeff and tells him, "Calm down and purchase the metal. We need to go."

Jeff glares at the merchant before lowering his hammer blaster. "You're lucky, young man." He slams the coins on the counter for the merchant, and the merchant heads back to gather the windomm.

Ophelia observes Roscoe as he looks out the shop's window. She walks over to him. "So, what was going on out there? You seemed to be looking for someone. You see something or someone?"

Roscoe brushed off her question as he walked away from the window. "No, nothing."

"Okay." She walks over to the window and looks out. She sees nothing, then looks back at him as he walks away, feeling like he is hiding something.

A soldier yells in the Command Center, "Captain on the Command deck!" The Command Center is a glass building above the city that controls the temperature, the lights, and the city's security. As they enter, everyone stands up and salutes Captain Mitchell and Razor.

"As you were," Cap replies.

Lt. Commander Buke approaches him. "Hello, Captain." Shaking his hand.

"Hello. Where is Commander Price, Lieutenant?" Captain Mitchell shakes his hand.

"She was feeling pretty run down, so she took the day off, sir," he says.

"Well, her children are headed that way. Hopefully, that will raise her spirits. So, what's the report on the fishing parties?"

"To be honest, sir, we have been obtaining fewer fish and even fewer squid nowadays." He hands him a tablet showing the data. "Since the crops are dying, the surplus need for fish is making the fishing parties return with less and less. Aquatic life around San-Van is becoming endangered, and the drop in surface water temperature is not helping either. They seem to be moving to warmer parts of Ma'de."

Cap looks at him in shock after seeing the numbers. "How much longer do we have?"

"Three years, give or take, if we are lucky, then the temperature dropping will make it where no more aquatic life can survive in this sector. The Norwest sector will be the only sector left and it's in the dark waters. Those are some treacherous waters to navigate due to the underwater volcano. It takes a true sailor to get through those treacherous waters. So, whatever you guys are going to do, you better come up with it soon."

"We will inform the emperor," Razor replies.

Captain Mitchell hands him the tablet back. "That's what we are here for. We came for some windomm. Ma'de's waters and the planet's crust make it the strongest metal in the galaxy. So, my team is getting that now. That's all I can say for now."

The Lieutenant nods. "I understand. I hope it works, Captain."

Captain Mitchell goes to leave. "Oh yeah. Where is Chancellor Riley? She asked to speak with me."

The Lieutenant looks up from the tablet and

answers, "She is at her estate. Should I let her know you are coming?"

"Yes, please," Captain Mitchell responds as they leave the Command Center. They take the elevator to the city level and get in a speeder.

A hologram shows up and asks, "Where to, sir?"

"To the Chancellor's estate, please," Cap replies.

"Very well," the hologram responds, and the speeder takes off down the street of San-Van.

"Man, I hate these civilian speeders. Having no way to control it is absurd." Razor folds his arms, shaking his head as he leans back in his seat.

Captain Mitchell snickers. "Every time, I figured you would be over this by now."

"I like to have the option just in case some shit goes down."

"Old friend, I have a question?" Captain Mitchell leans back in his seat. "Why do you think she summoned me to her estate?"

"I don't know. What do you think?"

"Jocelyn and I were very close once, but she is no different from the others. Be careful what you say, the Chancellors like to play word games to get what they want."

"Yes, Captain."

Captain Mitchell and Razor pull up to the front gate of the massive Chancellor's estate, which has a black gate around it and two guards standing at the front entrance. Captain Mitchell and Razor get out of either side of the speeder.

"Can I have your name, please, sir?" The guard asked as she approached them from the guard shack.

"Captain Mitchell. I have a meeting with the Chancellor."

"Let me see." The guard runs her fingers across the electronic pad. "Oh yeah, there you are. You are clear, sir." She waves them along and goes back to the shack.

"Thank you, soldier." Captain Mitchell responds.

They walk past the landscapers working on the shrubs in the shapes of the former Chancellors of Ma'de.

Razor smirks, looking at the shrubs. "I don't know if this is how I want to be remembered. A shrub in my image, just not what I pictured. What would you like Cap?"

"I'm not big on statues or anything like that. When I die, just scatter me with the stars where I belong."

Razor nods. "Roger, that Cap."

"What would you like, old friend?"

"I'm with you. Bury me on Osiris, where my forefathers lie."

"You got it. My friend."

They walk up to her door, and she opens it as they are about to knock. "Hello, Captain." A dark-skinned woman stands there. She is in her 40s, with white, blonde hair and a braid falling down her back to her waist. Her hair looks almost white compared to her dark blue Sari, which has beautiful seafoam-green Eyes of the Sea jewels down the spine of her dress.

"Hello, Chancellor Riley. What can I do for you?"

"How are you doing, Captain?" she replies,

stepping aside as they walk in.

"In the thick of it, trying to deal with this fish

issue, you know."

Her smile faded as they walked down the hall.

"That is why I have asked you here. The number of fish

is dwindling on Ma'de. You are closer to the Imperial

family than me. What have you been hearing? What are

the emperor's plans?"

"Jocelyn, we are trying to fix it, but I do not wish

to get in between the Chancellors and the Emperor. We

have bigger things to deal with than the politics of the

Imperial City."

She becomes intrigued. "What could be bigger

than our people starving?"

"You know I can't tell you that. What do you

want, Jocelyn?"

They stopped in front of her rose garden in the corridor, and a table set for three was ready.

She walks over to the table and sits. "I just want to know if we will survive this. The people are starving, and with starvation comes anarchy and chaos. We are fine for now, but I don't know how long it will take. To be honest, I'm afraid of what the future holds."

Captain Mitchell walks behind her and replies, "There is no need to worry. The emperor has a plan."

"I hope so. Does the Emperor ever intend to divulge his plan to us?"

He chuckles and says, "I don't know, but good try as I said, I cannot. That would be treason."

"Very well, then. Come join an old friend for some tea, won't you?" She gestures for him to sit with her.

Captain Mitchell looks at his watch. "Just for a second, we need to meet up with the rest of my team in the market." He sits at the table with her.

Razor sits down, rubbing his hands. "Good. I was eyeing that Pearl Squid. I heard it was to die for."

Luke and Lily ride in a speeder through their old neighborhood and see their childhood friend's house.

Lily looks out the window at the Mcdails' house. "Man, I wonder what happened to Hannah and Braxton? When was the last time you saw Hannah, Luke?"

Luke thinks for a bit. "Not since graduation night." They pull up to their parents' house. They exit the speeder and walk up to the door to a typical one-story San-Van house. Luke looks through the long living room window as Lily knocks on the door.

A few seconds later, a tall string bean of a man who resembled Luke answers the door. "My children! We've missed you. Come in!" Wrapping his arms around them and squeezing them tight before gesturing them inside. They walk inside, stepping on the glass floor as fish pass beneath their feet.

As they pass the bathroom, Luke stops. "I'll catch up. I must go pee. Too much to drink."

Lily and her father continue to the living room, where pictures of them as a family are on the wall. Some photographs of Lily by herself, some of Luke, and others of them together.

They cut between the TV and living room table and enter the kitchen. "Sit, sit. I have made some tea. Would you care for some?"

Lily pulls her chair from the square kitchen table and sits. "Yes, Father."

He turns to the shelf next to the stove and grabs three cups, setting them on the table as Luke walks up. He pours each cup before taking his seat across from them. "My children. You look amazing." He grabs their hands sobbing.

Lily is excited to see him. "So, how are things, Dad?

And where is Mom?"

"I'm doing okay, but your mom's not doing well. The food shortage has started hitting here, so we've been cutting back. Your mom, being who she is, has been giving her portion to the children in the neighborhood and not eating herself. It has taken a toll on her strength, so she's been exhausted, sleeping more." He takes a drink and then pauses. "Honestly, she's been saying some weird stuff here lately while sleeping."

Looking saddened by his appearance, Lily looks at her father, noticing he has grown thinner. "We will make this better, Father, I promise."

He takes a sip and says, "I know, baby girl. I am so proud of you two," a tear rolls down his cheek.

Luke thinks about what his father said, and his eyes widen, fearing what this could mean. "Dad, has she been taking her pills still?" When he finishes his sentence, their mother emerges from the back, holding their father's blaster pistol.

They all stand up and step back away from her.

"Martha, what are you doing? Hand me the blaster."
Their father holds his hand out.

She points it toward Lily, yells, "Long live The
Dream King!" and fires.

"Martha, no!" Their father screams, jumping in
between her and them just in time.

Luke flips over the table, yelling at Lily to get
down as their mother continuously fires at them. Luke
pulls Lily down as she frantically screams for her father.

A pool of his blood trickles towards her on the
floor as they watch their father say with his last breath,
"Forgive..."

They are trapped and helpless to do anything for
him.

Luke looks over at Lily and yells, "He is gone,
Lily. We must go!" Firing back towards his mom.

"It's Daddy!" she cries in utter shock as her father's blood mixes with her tears, rolling down her face.

"I know, and Mom is shooting at us! We must go now!" Their mother continues to shoot at them. "When she stops to reload, we jump out the window and get out of here to warn the others!" He yells to Lily. At the same time, he fires at his mom's feet to keep her back.

Soon after she stops firing to reload, he yells, "Now Lily!" She is frozen and does not want to leave her father's side. Luke grabs his sister, and they run through the living room. He shoots the window out and throws Lily down to the sidewalk. He fires at his mom and hops out the window. Just before he jumps, she fires back at him, hitting his shoulder and knocking him to the ground. He gets up and they start running towards the market.

Luke radios Captain Mitchell. "Captain, they are here, and my mother is now one of them. She killed my father. My father is dead." They ran up the sidewalk, passing people, not knowing who was going to turn on them next. "Lily, come on, we have to hurry and get off the streets."

The rest of the team hears this over comms and looks at each other in shock. Captain Mitchell replies, "Are you guys, ok?"

"We will be. I got shot in the shoulder. It's just a flesh wound, but Lily is pretty shaken up." He holds Lily up.

"Don't worry about coming here. Get back to the ship and secure our exit! I feel we will have to get out of here with haste."

Lily is so distraught about what happened that Luke practically carries her to the elevator.

Meanwhile, over in the market, Jeff, Ophelia, and Roscoe spot a group of The Dream Kings acolytes on the first level as they exit the metal shop. They appear to be searching for someone.

"Come on over here," Jeff says, walking to the other side of the shop to take cover in the alleyway.

Ophelia and Roscoe follow him. Once they cannot see them, she radios Cap and says, "We have some here, too. I'm going to say at least six." She peeks at them from behind the wall.

Captain Mitchell stands up and looks at Chancellor Riley. "I need you to send a squadron of troops to the western end of the market. We will come in from the east, trapping them in the middle. Hopefully, we can keep one alive this time."

Chancellor Riley was confused. "What is going on, Captain? What do you mean by this time?"

"My team and I have been dealing with these people. We will handle them; just shut down that side of the market."

"A lot is going on down there, Ray. It will take a lot for me to shut down that whole section." She stands up. "Who are these people?"

"I can't tell you; I just need you to do what I ask."

"I am the Chancellor of Ma'de. I order you to tell me!" an irritated Chancellor Riley yells.

"My orders come from a higher power than yours, and we are all here to serve him."

"Fine, I see how it is Ray, you owe me."

"Very well, but Razor and I will need a military speeder."

"You got it. I'll head to the Command Center and help from there."

"Thank you. I meant no disrespect earlier."

"Sure," she smirks as the doors to the Chancellor's estate open, and Captain Mitchell and Razor run out and get in one of her speeders.

A hologram comes up. "Where to sir?"

Razor pulls his seat belt down. "I will take the wheel, thank you." The steering wheel comes out of the dash.

They speed out of the circle drive and down the street with two other speeders following.

Down at the market, Ophelia tells Roscoe, "They are still searching for someone so stay close."

He nods. "Okay."

Jeff peeks from behind the wall. "They are at least then 30 feet away and closing. We have to move now."

"Okay, Roscoe, when we move, you move quickly and stay on my six," Ophelia tells him.

"I got you," Roscoe answers nervously.

"Okay, we are ready, Jeff. Let's move."

They all make their way back through the busy market, moving quickly, ducking down, hoping The Dream King's acolytes don't see them.

Luke and Lily reach the elevator, but no one is there. They board it and head towards the surface. In the elevator, Lily breaks down, still distraught.

Luke hugs her. "Lily, I know how you feel. We

will get that bastard for what he's done, but right now, I need you."

Lily, still entirely out of it, is unresponsive to Luke as she continues to sob. He yells again, "Lily, come on, bury it! I need you!"

She sniffles and wipes her face. "Okay, okay!" She stands up and loads her blaster. She notices his wound. "Are you okay, brother?"

He looks at his shoulder. "It just grazed me. I'll be fine." He loads his weapon. "Be ready."

Luke looks around the check-in station when they reach the top and exit the elevator. "Hey Cap, there's no one here."

"Go to the Dark Wolf and get it started," he replied.

They both say, "Yes, sir," and run out of station and up the dock to the Dark Wolf.

Captain Mitchell radios Ophelia, "We are at the eastern entrance and are moving towards the enemy."

Ophelia is hiding behind a crate. "Roger that, Cap. Okay, kid, we must make our way to the others." They come out from behind the crate. The Dream King acolytes notice Roscoe and open fires. They retake cover. "Jeff, do you have eyes on them?" The market becomes a madhouse with people running all over the place.

Jeff looks up from his cover on the other side of the market and says, "I don't have a clear shot! Too many people are in the way! Cap, we are going to need your help!"

Captain Mitchell radios Razor, "Do you have eyes on the enemy?"

"Yes, sir. Just keep them distracted." Razor running up from the east side.

Roscoe becomes anxious, falls to his knees, and feels a tingling sensation all over his body. He screams.

Ophelia bends down to check on him. "Hey kid, are you ok?"

Roscoe shoves her out of the way. "Get away from me!" His eyes turn blue, and he gets up and attacks one of the acolytes.

"Cap? Something is going on with this kid!"

"What do you mean?" Cap asked as he was taking fire himself.

"I don't know, something is happening to him."

"We will deal with it later, Ophelia, just keep him safe." Cap fires at one of the acolytes.

"Okay, but I don't think he needs it," she says as she watches him beat up the acolyte.

"Luke, Lily, do you see anything yet up there?" Cap fires at some acolytes.

"No, sir. Nothing is going on up here. Would you like me to come back?" Luke replies, looking at the Dark Wolf's bridge.

"Lt. Commander Buke, do you have anything on camera?" Cap orders.

"Yes, sir, they are moving towards the center and headed to the west, Captain."

"Are your men there yet?"

"No, they are about ten minutes out."

Roscoe powers up and yells, "I'm going to kill you!" He moves faster than the acolyte can see and punches him in the face. Then knee him in the stomach, causing him to fall.

The acolyte looks up at Roscoe. "Hello boy." A sinister, dark voice says through the acolyte.

"What the hell is going on?" Roscoe asks, picking up the man by his throat. "Leave me alone!" Roscoe punches the man in the chest, killing him before passing out. He is drained from using his powers.

Ophelia runs up to check on Roscoe as the rest of the acolytes disappear into the crowd.

"They are gone. Something is off. Keep your eyes peeled, guys," Cap orders as he helps a citizen to his feet. Jeff, do you have the windomm?" he asks as he looks around the market.

"Yes, sir," Jeff responds looking at the metal sheets in the corner.

"Okay, we got what we came for. Lt Commander, we will need medics down here, people are hurt. Team regroup at the drop-ship—over and out," Cap replies.

"Cap, Roscoe is out. I'll have to carry him."

Jeff walks up carrying the windomm. "I got them, Cap." Jeff pulled out his blaster.

Ophelia picked up Roscoe. "What's going on?" Roscoe mutters before passing back out.

Man, they had to have had a reason to be here. Luke thinks, still puzzled. Suddenly, he remembers not seeing a drop ship when they were running to theirs.

"Oh shoot," Luke says. He radioed Cap, "Captain, we must return to the station! They have a drop-ship."

The boat dock chief wakes from being knocked out by one of The Dream King's acolytes. He says to the Lt. Commander, "Commander, he is right. They attacked me, knocked me out, and stole a code for one of the drop-ships, sir."

"Are you ok, chief?" Lt. Buke says.

"Yes, Sir. My records show we should have sixteen drop-ships on this side of the port, and we only have fifteen." He puts an ice pack on.

Captain Mitchell shouts, "Everyone, we have to get to the Dark Wolf now!" They all begin to run.

Luke radios the Lt. Commander and says, "I'll let you know when we have reached the station."

"Roger that," Lt. Commander Buke replies.

As they run, Dr. Beal radios them and tells them they're being fired upon by a ship.

"We are hurrying now," Captain Mitchell says to Dr. Beal but loses the connection with her. "Luke, what is happening? Try the Station again."

"Dr. Beal, this is the Dark Wolf over," but nothing. "I got nothing, sir. We need to hurry and get up there," Luke replied.

"On our way!" He yells as he and the team run through the market to the elevator. Cap and the rest of the team get to the Dark Wolf and climb back on. Cap runs in, presses the button next to the door, sealing the pressure in the ship, and orders, "Luke, take off, get us out of here now! I'll be on the bridge in a minute. Ophelia, take Roscoe to the medical bay."

"Yes, captain."

"Lily, retract the anchor now," she doesn't respond. Luke looks over at her, she is back in a state again, staring off into nothingness. "Lily!" Luke yells, "Lily, I know we have so much going on, but I need you. Lil!" She doesn't respond. "Cap, she is still compromised right now. Randi, start the ship, and I'll retract the anchor myself."

Captain Mitchell enters the bridge. "Luke, what

happened?"

"My mom was not taking her pills, and he got her. She came out of the back with my dad's blaster and shouted, 'Long live The Dream King,' then fired at us. My father jumped in the way to save us, and she killed him. They used my family and the market to distract us so they could take a drop-ship from right underneath our noses. What would they need more drop-ships for?"

"Shit! I can't imagine anything good." Captain Mitchell, furious as he sits in his seat, "We got played!" He slams his fists onto the arm of his Captain's seat. He sighs and sees Luke's wound. "You need to get that shoulder looked at."

I'll be fine for now, sir," Luke responds while wrapping a bandage around the wound.

Roscoe awakes in the medical bay. "What the hell is going on?" he yells.

Ophelia says, "We are under attack. You need to lay back down so the pod can scan you."

Roscoe gets out worried about Henry. "I'm fine. I'm leaving. My friend is up there!" Roscoe gets dressed and leaves the medical bay. Ophelia follows him.

He storms onto the bridge. "What are we doing? Why are we still here?"

Lily snaps, turns around in her co-pilot seat, and tells Roscoe, "Calm down. I understand that he means a lot to you but sit down. I promise we got this." She has tears in her eyes.

He looks at her, feeling terrible and calms down. "I am so sorry. I know, but you guys are used to this. Henry and I are not."

Captain Mitchell says, "I can promise you he's okay." He assures him. "We have the best team. They will protect him."

"So, what's taking us so long to leave?" Roscoe asked.

"We must sail from the city to the takeoff line."

"Okay then." Roscoe goes and takes his seat with

the rest of the crew.

"Okay," Captain Mitchell says, "Take us out, Randi."

"Roger, sir"

Luke reaches out and grabs Lily's hand. Seeing her wipe tears from her eyes. "We will kill them all, I promise."

She sobs. "I know, brother." Her face changes to a scowl. "I Know."

Captain Mitchell, unsure what awaits them, says, "Randi, turn the shield on. We don't know what we are about to deal with."

"Got it." The sails come down, and the shield goes up.

"Let's go," Captain Mitchell orders. The ship starts to move. Lily and Luke sail to the take-off line and jet into outer space.

"Luke."

"Yes, Cap?" He responded looking back.

"As soon as we are in range, try radioing them again." Cap leans back in his seat, looking out the window.

"Roger that," Luke answers.

When the Dark Wolf reaches the upper atmosphere of Ma'de, Luke radios the station. "Dr. Beal, come in. This is the Dark Wolf. Over." He does not receive a response, so he tries again. "Dr. Beal, this is the Dark Wolf. Over."

"Why are they not answering?" Cap becomes worried.

Luke is confused as well. "Maybe we are not in range yet. We should be able to see them when we get out of Ma'de's atmosphere."

When they reach the outer atmosphere of Ma'de, the station is not there. Fragments of the station were floating around. Luke looks back at Cap worried. "Where are they, sir?"

Captain Mitchell tells Lily, "Do a deep scan to see if they are near."

She scans for them. "No, sir, nothing!"

"Okay." He leans back rubbing his goatee. *I wonder where they went. Dang it, doctor, what are you doing?* He thinks. "It's okay. We were planning on heading to Osiris next. We will head that way, and hopefully, they will be there."

Roscoe stands up. "Wait, we are just going to go on without them."

"Yes, Dr. Beal and I reviewed the plan last night, so she knows where we are going. They did what they thought was right and we must trust them."

"Okay, very well then." Roscoe goes to exit the bridge and whispers to himself. "Henry, I hope you are ok."

"You think he will be, okay?" Lily asks.

Cap responds, "I'll talk to him. Are you okay, Lily?"

"I'll be okay," she says as she wipes more tears, looking more level-headed now.

"Okay, then, Randi." He walks to the map in the center of the screen and brings up a hologram of the planets.

Randi responds, "Yes, Captain?"

"Set a course for Osiris. We plan to head there for a power core."

"Okay, Captain," she says, and the Dark Wolf takes off.

Captain Mitchell gets on the intercom. "We will have a team meeting in the Chow Hall at 1600, and Roscoe, meet me at my quarters in five minutes. The rest of you shower up and get some rest. That is all for now." He hangs up and looks over at Luke and Lily. "I'm so sorry for your loss, guys. You can let Randi take over the autopilot and take some time to yourselves."

"Yes, sir." They both reply.

Captain Mitchell leaves the cabin and walks to his

quarters. On his way to his room, he runs into Ophelia.

"Cap, I need to tell you something." Ophelia was

not quite sure what she saw. "I know you gotta talk to

the kid but let me tell you something. When we were

down on Ma'de before everything happened, Roscoe

acted weird in the market. —as if he was seeing

someone, but I couldn't get a beat on them and his eyes

changed and glowed all blue when he was fighting."

"That is very interesting." He rubs his goatee.

"Thanks, Ophelia, I'll bring it up when I speak with

him."

"He seems like a good kid, but he's hiding something

from us. I'll let you go, Cap. I need to go check on Lily."

"Yes, he does. Let me know how Lily is doing, ok?

She will talk to you."

"I will," she replies before walking down the hallway

towards Lily's quarters.

When Captain Mitchell arrives, Roscoe is waiting for

him at his door. "Hey, kid, come on in." He places his hand

on the pad on the wall, and the door opens

"Thanks, Captain," Roscoe replies as he enters the

room. Cap follows.

Roscoe walks around Captain Mitchell's quarters,

noticing they are much bigger and better than the one he

was sleeping in. In the center of the room is a table with two

chairs and a large bed behind it. In the corner is a desk with

a computer and record player. "When can I get a room like

this?" Roscoe laughs and shakes his head.

Captain Mitchell watches him and chuckles. "When

you become Captain, you will."

Roscoe leans over, admiring the white record player

with a golden rose and the initials R&K4L. "You believe I

can be?"

Captain Mitchell pulls out a chair. "I believe you are

going to do great things. Now, can you sit down? We have a

lot to discuss." He hangs his uniform jacket in his locker

and places the record player's needle onto a record, and soft music begins to play. "I saw you looking at it. Do you like music?"

Roscoe sits down. "Yes, a little."

Captain Mitchell walks over to his nightstand and notices Roscoe's hand is trembling and bruised. "Yeah, an old friend gave me that." He puts his stuff from his pockets on top of his nightstand. "Are you hungry? A lot was going on at once down there. Most people get hungry once the adrenaline wears off." He walks over to his desk, pulls a power bar out, and tosses it to Roscoe. Then, he sits at the table with him as he scarfs it down. "Good huh?" Captain Mitchell smiles.

Roscoe looks up at him and says between chews, "No, but you were right. I did need this. It's not enough though. I could still eat a hole Cockapee."

Captain Mitchell chuckles. "Don't worry, after this and the meeting, dinner should be ready. Ophelia is making her famous Fury chili tonight, which is the best."

"Okay good." Roscoe takes the last bite of the power bar. "So, Captain, do you know what has happened to Henry and the station yet?"

"I don't know, but I promise he is safe, and Dr. Beal will do everything to keep him that way."

"What do you mean she will keep him safe? I thought he was supposed to be keeping her safe."

He laughs and loads tobacco in his pipe. "He will be fine. I promise."

"Okay, I want to believe you, but I'm worried about him. We have not been apart this long before, sir."

"Trust me for now. That's all I got for you, kid." Captain Mitchell calmly tells him. "So, we need to talk about what happened down there, and who were you looking at?"

"Ophelia told you about that, huh," Roscoe responds.

"Yeah, she said you seemed off. Everything ok?"

"Yes, it's just that I thought I saw someone, but then they were gone," Roscoe states.

"Through a purple cloud of smoke?" Captain Mitchell takes a puff on his pipe.

"Yes," Roscoe said. "How did you know?"

"We've contacted her multiple times, but she always seems to escape us through a purple cloud of smoke."

"Do you know who she is?" Roscoe asked.

"I don't." Captain Mitchell tells him. "But I will help you find out. Right now, you just have to trust me, okay?"

"Okay. Thank you." Roscoe says.

"You're welcome. Also, Ophelia said your eyes turned blue. Do you know anything about that?"

Roscoe is confused. "What are you talking about, Cap?"

"You don't remember anything that happened at the market."

"No, nothing. After we were surrounded, sir, I

figured I had tripped running away and knocked myself out. I can be clumsy like that sometimes."

"No, something else happened. Ophelia said you were glowing and killed one of the acolytes yourself."

"Sir, I do not remember what you are talking about."

"Nothing at all."

"Sir, nothing at all."

Captain Mitchell was confused and intrigued by him. "Very interesting, well enough with all that work talk. Let's get some food. It's been a long day."

"Okay, I'm hungry but want to check on Lily first. I will meet you there, sir."

"Okay, but don't be too long," Captain Mitchell tells him. It's first come, first serve."

They leave Captain Mitchell's quarters and head toward the chow hall. Roscoe stops by Lily's room. He raises his fist as it shakes, becoming nervous even to knock. He shakes it off and knocks on her door, excited to see her.

When the door opens, he sees Lily, her eyes still red and swollen from crying. "Hi," she says.

"Hi, I just wanted to check in on you, but I can return later."

"No, it's okay." She sniffles. "Come in. Would you like some water? I got some in here somewhere." Lily leaves the door open, and Roscoe walks in.

"Yes, thank you." Roscoe looks at her books, a toy model drop-ship, and other things while he waits for her.

Lily walks over to her desk and moves something aside. "There you are." She finds the pack of water and hands him one.

"Thank you."

"You're welcome. So, what did you want to tell me?" She walks over to her locker, throws her blood-stained shirt to the floor, and grabs another.

Roscoe turns his back to her. "Oh yeah. I just wanted

to let you know if you need someone to talk to, I'm here. I

know how hard it is to lose parents."

"Thank you, Roscoe, that is so kind of you, and I'm

sorry to hear that about your parents, Roscoe." She placed

her hand on his shoulder so he could turn back around.

"No need, that was long ago, and I have accepted it."

"I'm not trying to pry, but what happened to them, if

you don't mind talking about it," she asks, sitting down.

"It is ok. To be honest, I don't know." Roscoe sits

down next to her and opens his water.

"What do you mean?"

"I grew up at Saint Ethel's Boy's Home, and they had

no idea who my family was. Someone just dropped me off

there, and they didn't leave anything, just a paper with my

name on it."

"I'm sorry that happened to you, Roscoe," Lily,

feeling awful about what happened, places her hand on his.

"Hey, don't be sorry for me. I've had an okay life,

and I got Henry out of it," he replies.

"You guys are pretty close, huh?"

"Thick as thieves. I hope he is okay," Roscoe replies.

"That's awesome. That is how Ophelia and I are; she is my best friend, and I would feel the same. I promise you he will be okay."

"Thank you, well enough about me, how are you doing?" he asked concernedly.

Lily gets choked up and a tear rolls down her cheek. "It just doesn't feel real. Like a piece of me is missing and I don't know what to do with that."

"I'm so sorry, Lily. It hurts now, but remember they are always with you."

She hugs him and Roscoe turns red. "Thank you so much for the advice." Roscoe's stomach growls. "Are you hungry?"

"Yes, extremely. I hear Ophelia's Fury Chili is amazing. Would you like to go get some with me?"

She stands up. "It is. Give me a minute to clean up my mess, and then we can go."

"I'll step out and give you a minute." he heads for the door.

"Thank you. I'll be out in a sec," Lily responds. She stares at him as he walks out the door, thinking, "Was he that handsome yesterday?"

Roscoe is standing outside Lily's room, staring into outer space, wondering how his life got to this point. A few days ago, he was working at a plant. Now, he's in outer space. He laughs, "I cannot believe I'm on a drop-ship in outer space. " He is in awe of the beauty of space.

The door opens, and Lily is in a jumpsuit with a black tank top, the arms of her jumpsuit tied around her waist. She came out with her hair parted down the middle and braided pigtails. Her two braids fall over both shoulders.

She looks terrific, Roscoe thought while staring in awe and fear simultaneously.

"Let's go eat," she said before walking past him towards the chow hall.

They both walk down the Dark Wolf's winding halls, unable to keep their eyes off each other. They reach the last entrance on their left and enter the chow hall. When they arrive, everyone else is already there. In the middle of the room is a long table with chairs on the sides and a full kitchen.

Standing over the stove, Ophelia says, "You guys made it finally. I'm just about done." She throws some potatoes into a pot. "How about you, Jeff, with that salad?" she looks over her shoulder at him.

"I got it, I got it, don't worry about me I'm almost done." Jeff cuts some green tomatoes and throws them into a bowl.

Lily leans over to Roscoe and says, "Jeff loves to eat but can't cook." She chuckles. "That's the only thing we let him make."

"Is he bad at it?" Roscoe asks.

"He likes his spices." She chuckles.

"That's an understatement," Ophelia says and laughs.

"Wow, what is that amazing smell?" Roscoe asks.

"That's the chili." She takes a deep breath "Mm smells great O."

"Thanks. Hopefully, it's my best yet," Ophelia replies, stirring the chili.

She nudged him, and they watched Jeff splash some sauce onto the salad. "See, that's why. He always makes everything extremely spicy, and only he can eat it." Lily laughed, thinking about all the times they had tried his cooking, and immediately regretted it, watching everyone spit it out and run for water.

Roscoe laughs and says, "You look good when you smile."

Lily blushes. "Thanks."

Jeff, walking to the table with the salad, says to Roscoe, "Come over here by me, Casanova." Roscoe walks over and sits next to Jeff. "So, kid, what kind of sauce do you want with your chili? Mild, hot, or my favorite, kick

your ass hot?"

"I'll just stick with the mild thanks," he said.

They all laugh. Captain Mitchell says, "Good choice.

Let the boy be now. Give me the mild Jeff." He smiles at

Roscoe.

As everyone chows down on their Fury chili, Roscoe

asks while slurping down a spoonful.

"Why are all the chairs on the side and none at the

head of the table?"

Razor responds, "I got this. Captain Mitchell sees us

as a family, so no one is better than the other, and no one

sits at the head of the table. We eat together as a family."

Captain Mitchell stands up and says, "It should take

us four days to get to Osiris, so Roscoe, eat up. Tomorrow,

we start training." Then he holds up his drink and his

expression sadden. "We lost a good man today. Let's raise

our glasses." Everyone raises their glass. "David Price was a

great man and friend but an even better father. Lily, Luke,

your dad was very proud of you two, don't forget it. So, here's to him. May we meet in the stars."

"May we meet in the stars," they all repeat and take a drink.

He walks to the sink and puts his bowl down. He turns back around and says, "Jeff, it's your night to do the dishes. Ensure it gets done; don't drink too much and forget."

"Yes, sir, I won't. Night, sir!" Jeff responds.

"Night, Cap!" they all say as he leaves the room.

Lily dries her eyes, looks at Ophelia, and says, "You got more of that tea? I need some sleep."

"I do; it's in my room. Let's go, and I'll give you some." Ophelia responds, arms draped around Lily's shoulders

"Well, then I'm going to bed too. Training sounds fun," Roscoe said.

Jeff says, "It's early, kid. Where are you going? Have a drink with me."

Lily and Ophelia get up from the table and say to Roscoe over their shoulder as they go to put their dish up. "Don't do it, Roscoe. One will turn into many!"

"Don't listen to them. Man up, come on!" Jeff grabs his drink from the cabinet.

Roscoe is unsure of what he wants to do—wondering if he will see the woman again if he does. ""Fine, I'll have one, but that's it. Night, Lily," he says.

"Night, have fun." She shakes her head as she and Ophelia leave.

Razor reaches over with a tin cup. "One for me, and don't forget training is at 0400. Night, gentleman." He whistles as he leaves the chow hall with the cup in hand.

"So, it's just the three of us then," Jeff says, referring to himself, Roscoe, and Luke.

"Nope, gotta keep this figure. I'm going to work out. I need to clear my head as well. Later." He leaves with a bottle of this green liquid from the fridge.

Jeff slides a cup over to Roscoe. "Looks like it's just

you and me," as he pours Roscoe a drink.

Roscoe watches him, humming a tune as he pours. "So, I mean, no disrespect, but you seem more down-to-earth and carefree than I have heard about your kind."

"Yeah, that's not all of us, I learned to live my life one day at a time," Jeff says to Roscoe, taking a sip.

"I am not trying to be rude, but are you not Rydeanin? Do you guys not live forever?" Roscoe asks with a confused expression on his face.

"No, Roscoe that is just a rumor. Everyone lives and everyone dies. Our life spans are just longer than yours. For every fifty years of your life, it's only five years of ours."

"Oh wow! That's a good way to live. You have seen a lot huh?"

"Yes, but not everyone sees it that way. My father has always hated the lifestyle I chose. You see, I'm a five-generation imperial soldier. My father was, and his father was before him, and so on. I am somewhat of a legacy." He takes a drink. "My father was in line to be Admiral, and the emperor gave the position to the Empress. During the rebellion of Lavander Half-hand on Osiris, and my older brother died. He never forgave the emperor for making her Admiral, so he retired and now wants to tell me how to live my life. Afraid I will die on another planet serving the emperor's cause. I say I live by the sword. I will die by the sword, and I will have fun doing it. I'm still here, so there's that, bud, slapping Roscoe on the back, taking a big gulp.

Roscoe lifts his glass and says, "I can drink to that. Be your own man." He takes a drink and immediately starts coughing. After he stops, he says, "What the hell is this, man?"

Jeff chuckles. "It's my brew made from berries, potato skins, and an elixir I got from Newwart." Roscoe and Jeff laugh and continue to drink.

Roscoe becomes drunk. "Wow! That means you were alive during the Reign of Orin the Great!" Roscoe hiccups.

"Yes, I joined the Cleat Academy at the end of his reign. Thinking about it now, I think that was the last time I saw my dad smile. He was so proud of me." Jeff takes a drink.

"Family is overrated. Look at Henry and me; we have been like brothers since we met. Family isn't always blood. You know what they say? 'The blood of the covenant is thicker than the water of the womb.'"

Jeff chuckles, grabs Roscoe by the neck, and rubs his head, spilling their drinks. "You're wiser than your years, kid. I'll give you that."

Roscoe pulls away, chuckling. He fixes his hair and takes another drink. "Thanks."

A few hours later, Jeff realizes how late it is and how toasty Roscoe has become. "Hey, kid, let's call it a night. You've got an early morning ahead of you."

Roscoe slurs his words, swaying back and forth. "Okay, sounds good."

Jeff lifts Roscoe and lets him lean on him as he walks down the hallway to his room. When they arrive, Roscoe tells Jeff, "Man, thanks for the drinks. It was fun, and it got my mind off worrying about Henry. It's nice to have someone else to hang out with. I don't have many friends, so thank you."

Jeff opens Roscoe's door and lays him on his bed. Roscoe plops down, reaching his arm with a closed fist and looking for a fist bump.

Jeff laughs, bumps Roscoe's fist, and tells him, "Goodnight, kid. It was my pleasure. Good luck tomorrow." He leaves and shuts the door behind him.

As Roscoe falls asleep, he begins to Dream Weave, seeing someone's dream through their eyes.

The soldier radios. "Drop-ship Falcon 20, respond." Nothing happens, but he hears it again: "Falcon 20, respond."

A familiar woman's voice comes over the coms. "Long live The Dream King!" Then a Cannon fire goes off. Boom! Boom! The Falcon fires at Federation Station, hitting it dead on and knocking out part of its communications, radar, and weaponry systems.

Dr. Beal stumbles onto the bridge as alarms are going off. "What the heck was that?

"We are under attack, Ma'am," the soldier responds.

"Get Captain Mitchell on the comms now!"

"Yes, ma'am, calling him now."

"Cap, this is The Dark Wolf over."

"This is Captain Mitchell, over."

"Cap, we are under attack. We have been ambushed." They get hit again and lose connection.

"Cap, Cap!" Doctor Beal yells.

"We lost them Doc."

"How bad is it?" Dr. Beal asked, trying to assess the situation.

"We have no weapons, the long-range comms are out, and the radar is spotty, ma'am. We won't be able to reach the others again," the soldier tells her.

"Who would be foolish enough to steal from the Empire?" she says, looking at the drop ship behind them.

"Falcon 20, this is Dr. Beal of the Izealin Federation Station 2625. In the name of the emperor, you are under arrest."

"Haha, Hello Brooklyn, I'm glad you are there," Rachel responds in a sinister voice over the coms.

"Damn you, Rachel! What game are you playing? What do you want?" Dr. Beal asks just as Henry enters the bridge.

"It's not what I want. It's too late for that. She stole that from me. It's what he wants, and that's Roscoe," She replies as she walks up and down the bridge of her ship.

"What is going on?" Henry said. Wait, what did she say? Is that the same woman Roscoe was talking about earlier?" He fired question after question at Dr. Beal.

Dr. Beal yells at him. "Not now, Henry! I'll explain later. Right now, we've gotta get out of here."

Rachel comes back over the coms and says, "I'm going to give you ten seconds to give the boy to me, or you and every soul on that ship is going to die, and then I will just take him."

Dr. Beal pauses and says, "Rachel, don't do this!" trying to stall her. Looking at Henry, she says, "She thinks he is with us, so we must draw her away from the others."

Henry says, "What about Roscoe? We can't!"

"She has cut off our way to retreat to San-van. We have to go. It is for the best. She can't have him." She responds.

"What are you saying? We can't just leave him. I'm all Roscoe has!" Henry says frantically.

Dr. Beal shakes Henry. "Calm down, Henry. He will be okay, I promise. We have to go now."

The soldier says, "We have to get out of here. She has weapons locked in on us."

"Get the shield up, and we will pull them away from the team," Dr. Beal replies.

Henry asks, "Where do we go?"

"Back to Izeal. We can fix the station there," she says.

"We are too far away, ma'am. The shield won't last," a soldier yells.

"Then how about Newwart?" she says.

"By my recollection, Ma'am, Captain Kasie should be patrolling around Newwart's moon. That should work, ma'am," he replies.

"Set a course for Newwart. Maybe we can set a trap for her and repair our ship there."

"Roger that, Ma'am. Randi set a course for the Highyeah Mountains."

"I am on it," Randi replies.

"Are they following us?" Dr. Beal asked.

"Yes," The pilot responds.

"Ok, keep her close," Dr. Beal says as they lead them away from Ma'de.

At that very moment, Rachel senses Roscoe's presence in the soldier. "I see you, boy. He is not with them. Change our course for Osiris now!"

Chapter 3

Roscoe awakes to Razor shouting and banging on his door. "Rise and shine!"

He sits in bed, half asleep and hungover from the previous night. He tries to catch his breath. "*Did I just dream that, or was that happening?*" He thinks to himself.

Razor knocks again. "Let's go kid! Get a move on it."

Roscoe sighed, got up, opened the door, rubbed his head, and saw Razor standing with a cup of coffee. "Shoot, you don't have to be so loud. My head feels like it's been split open."

Razor sips his coffee and laughs. "Yeah, he gave you the good stuff. We better get some chow in you before we start. I have something for that, too. Come on, follow me."

"Roger, that sergeant, let me get dressed real quick." He returns to his room and puts on his Izealian training uniform. It's a gold T-shirt, black pants, and jogging shoes.

He returns to the hallway. "Okay, I'm ready."

"Took you long enough. Chows going to be cold."

"Sorry, sergeant. I'm still getting used to the locker."

He and Razor head to the chow hall to grab some food before beginning their training for the day.

Captain Mitchell and Luke walks into the chow hall ahead of them and Luke smarts off. "Dang my boy, you look awful."

Captain Mitchell looks back at Roscoe and chuckles. "Good night, huh?"

Roscoe's stomach rumbles, and he tries not to throw up. "Awe, yes, sir, but I regret it today."

Cap chuckles as they stand in line for food. Behind Roscoe in line, Razor replies, "I got him, Cap, I'm going to give him my hangover cure. He will be ready for the training simulator before we leave."

"Good, I want to see what he's got." Cap nods at Roscoe.

Roscoe feels a sense of pride and is ready to go. "So, what's for chow?"

"Eggs and potatoes are what we have left," Ophelia replies.

Roscoe says, "No more Fury?"

"Nope, we will not have more meat till we get to Osiris."

"Dang it, that meat was good, " he replies, grabbing his stomach as it growls again.

Luke says, "Here you go, buddy, we told you." Laughing at him while he hands him his scrambled eggs and fried potatoes.

He walks over to the table and sits down. Roscoe takes a bite and then turns to Captain Mitchell. "Have you heard anything about Henry and the Space Station yet?"

"No, hopefully, I will hear something soon. I'll tell you something at the briefing later this morning." Captain Mitchell replied.

"Okay thank you, sir." He continues to eat, thinking

about what he saw, still uncertain if it was real.

Lily walks into the chow hall and to the fridge. "So, Roscoe, are you ready for the simulator?" She looks into the refrigerator, holding a protein bar and a towel around her neck, her hair still wet from the shower.

Roscoe smiles at her then takes a bite. "Yeah, so what's it like?"

Jeff gets up from the table laughing. "Buckle up, young fella, it's about to be one heck of a ride."

Ophelia says, "Should we tell everyone how your first time went, Jeff?"

"No, no, no." he quickly replies.

Lily says, "Don't listen to him. I'll tell you the truth. If you get hit, you will feel a shock. It pushes your body farther than it can on Newwart at the Academy, so you get better faster. I promise you; you work out a couple of times in the simulator, and your mind and body will be ready for what lies ahead of us."

Roscoe finishes his food and says, "Sergeant, I'm

ready for your hangover cure."

"Okay then." Razor gets up, goes over, grabs some things from the cabinets, and concocts a drink. He places it down in front of Roscoe. "You have to drink the whole thing."

Roscoe gulps down the whole thing and makes a disgusted face. "Oh, my that was nasty." He stretches. "But man, I feel better already."

"Good, you should be recovered enough to start." Razor nods, standing over him.

Captain Mitchell turns to Razor. "Before you guys start, let's meet on the bridge in five minutes."

"Yes, sir!" they all reply.

"Roscoe, you also have dishes today. Welcome to the crew," he says, and they all laugh as Cap walks out of the chow hall.

Roscoe looks back and sees the sink full. He sighs, drops his head, and walks out. "Dang it, guys!"

When they all reach the bridge and circle the center

monitor island, Cap presses a button that brings up holographs of all the planets. He hits Osiris, which enhances the holograph, showing the number of people, they believe are living on Osiris and its Chancellor, Amri Graves.

Luke says, "Hey Cap, any word about our mom?"

Captain Mitchell shakes his head. "Sorry, guys. I got a call from Chancellor Riley, and your mom left with all the rest of The Dream King's acolytes. We have no clue where they have gone. I'm so sorry, guys."

Lily optimistically says, "That means she can still be alive."

"No, Lily." Luke snaps. "She's dead to us now! How could you even care about her after what she did? Father is dead, and I have a hole in my shoulder because of her."

"Luke, ease yourself, my friend." Jeff put his hand on Luke's arm. Luke yanks away and storms off, and Jeff goes after him.

Captain Mitchell reassures Lily. "We will find your mom,

Lily, I promise, but we must stay on mission for now. We will go to Osiris and to the city of Ojacka to find a smuggler named Tekey-Espy. They say he spends much of his time at a bar downtown called Meg's."

Razor says, "I know Meg. We go way back from before she became a Thug Lord. She should help us."

Captain Mitchell continues, "Ok, good that should help. Tekey-Espy has a power core that we need for the portal. We will come up with a plan when we get there. We have two days before we arrive at Osiris. That's all I have for today."

Roscoe says, "So hey, Cap, any word on Henry and the others?"

Captain Mitchell shakes his head. "I'm sorry, Roscoe, I still haven't heard from them. I'm sure they will pop up soon. He is just fine, don't worry."

Razor says, "Well, kid, let's start your training."

"It's okay. Just let me know when you do, Cap." He is unsure of what he saw in his dream and doesn't know if he should bring it up with him, so he dismisses it. "Ok then, Let's go, Sergeant. I'm excited to see what it is all about." Roscoe replied.

"You got this and remember to make sure you duck."

"Yes, sir, and see you later, Lily," he says as he runs off to catch up with Razor.

Lily giggles. "Okay, see ya Roscoe."

Ophelia and Lily head out behind them to Ophelia's room. Once inside, Ophelia and Lily sit on the bed with Lily between Ophelia's legs as she braids her hair. "Lil, I'm so sorry about your dad."

They hug and Lily tells her "My mother just killed my father. I'm dreaming, right? Did that really happen?"

Ophelia grabs Lily as they both tear up, wrapping her arms around her and hugging her again. "I'm here for you always! I'm so sorry!"

Lily cries and answers, "I don't know what to do. Luke and I are losing it, and I don't know how to fix it."

"Stay strong sister, we will help you guys through this."

"Thank you so much." Ophelia starts to braid her hair again.

"So, what do you think of Roscoe?" Ophelia asks Lily.

"He was there for me and gave me some good advice."

Ophelia looks down at her and replies. "You sure it's not his looks?" They giggle. "I saw how you looked at each other the other night."

Lily starts to blush. "Yeah, he is kinda cute." She laughs.

"There is something off about him, though. I feel like he is hiding something," Ophelia said.

"He just had a rough childhood and doesn't trust easily, O? You, of all people, can understand that" Lily added.

"Yeah, you are right. Fine, but I'm watching him."

"I have no doubt you will, but I think I can handle him myself," she smiles as she considers him.

"Do you like him or something?" Ophelia asks.

Lily's face turns red with embarrassment. "I don't know."

"Uh-huh." Ophelia jokes.

Lily changes the subject saying, "Luke is pretty pissed off at our mom."

"Yeah, he is. Are you not?" Ophelia asks.

"No." Lily becomes angry. "I'm pissed at The Dream King and his acolytes. They are the cause of my family's pain, and I will make them all pay."

"We will get what we need to get there and save her and everyone else."

"I know, I just hope my mom is okay when we do," Lily whispered.

"She will be, my dear friend," Ophelia replies, embracing her again.

Meanwhile, Luke and Jeff are in the chow hall playing a game of chess. "Knight takes the pawn," Luke says to Jeff.

"So, what's up, buddy?"

"Nothing." Luke, are we going to talk about what happened to your dad and what you said? That was some heavy shit, brother."

Luke says, "Not right now, man. I just want to play for now and find what we need to kill them all and The Dream King."

Jeff raises his eyebrows. "Your mom is with them." Jeff makes a move.

"She is not my mother anymore," Luke replies, irritated. Maybe you should pay more attention to the game, and you won't be losing."

"Luke, what if we can't find a builder? They say the builders were outlawed from teaching their ways. We don't know exactly where to find one."

As Jeff moves his pawn in the game, Luke tells him, "It's Cap. He always has a plan."

"I understand that, Luke, but you cannot let revenge consume you, my friend. It will kill you," Jeff says.

"You have no idea what I feel right now! Your dad is just a dick. Mine is dead!" he yells, and he shoves the pieces onto the floor and storms off.

"Dang, it's like that, huh?" Jeff says, pulling his flask out and taking a sip as Luke walks out of sight.

Razor asks Roscoe in the training room, "Are you ready to get hooked up?" At the bottom of the ship is a big workout room with benches, dumbbells, and other workout equipment. Four helmets, each with a glass face shield that pulls down over their faces, hang in front of a tall glass mirror along the wall.

Roscoe replies, "What are those?" and points at the helmets hanging from the ceiling.

"Ah, yes," the old man said, "That is what we will be

hooking up to."

"Oh…" his eyes got wide with excitement. "I'm ready!" he exclaimed.

"Okay, first, we will start by getting you into shape. The obstacle course should do," Razor says to him. They put on their helmets.

Roscoe pulls his shield down and sees Razor standing there, but they are outside, surrounded by beautiful trees and a vibrant blue sky. He was from Izeal, and he'd never seen trees before, so he was amazed at how enormous and green they truly were. He continued to look around. He sees an obstacle course in front of them.

The starting line appears in front of them. "Let's work. Remember," Razor says, "If you fall, you feel a shock. You get hit, you feel a shock, and as this happens, your body will adapt faster here, so the more you train, the faster your body and mind will improve. Ready? Set. GO!" Roscoe takes off, running up the ladder. He gets knocked off by a swinging pad coming out of nowhere. He feels a shock to his body.

"Hell, Sgt, that hurt," he says as he rolls on the ground.

"Get up and do it again! Now you know."

Roscoe gets up and does it again. This time when the pole swings at him, his eyes glow blue again, and his instincts take over, but neither he nor Razor notices at the moment.

Razor meets him at the end with Roscoe bent over, huffing and puffing. "How was that?" he gasped.

"Randi, what was his time?" Razor asks the computer.

Randi responds in a female voice, "Four minutes and fifteen seconds."

Razor turns to Roscoe. "Wow! That's amazing for your first time. Let's get that down to three minutes," he says, feeling confident he can do it.

"Let's go!" Roscoe is excited but out of breath.

"You got this. Lift your head, get your breath, and we will go again." Razor states.

"Did all of you do this, sergeant?" Roscoe asks as he catches his breath.

"Yes, kid, but ours was at the base on Newwart. Because of the mountains and snow, they have, it gives us harsher terrain to train on."

"I've never been to Newwart," Roscoe says. "Honestly, until a few weeks ago, I had never left Izeal."

"Yeah, I'm sorry, kid, that this is happening to you," Razor says. "You remind me of another kid I know."

"Ophelia?" Roscoe responds.

"Yes. You are much more observant than we have given you credit for. Keep that up; it will greatly help you in this business."

"Yes, sergeant," Roscoe replies. "It's a thing I do. I have been overlooked my whole life. People don't normally notice me. I have done it since I was a little boy. I watched many people go about their day from the roof of the boy's home as they passed by. Wondering if they were my family," he adds as his tone saddens.

"Dang kid, you have had it rough. Well, then, this might hit home for you. As I said, I was on Newwart because the mountain tribes rebelled. One night, while on patrol in the Highyeah mountains, I found her walking alone in the snow. Her parents were found dead in their home. Her father was the Chancellor in waiting, and her mother was the daughter of a mountain tribe chief. To this day, it is still unclear what happened, but the emperor couldn't let a Chancellor's murder go unchecked. So, he had us hunt down the mountain tribes and kill them or make them submit to Izealin law. After that, Emperor Noah built a training base there so that there would always be an Izealin military presence on Newwart to keep them in line. Ophelia had no one, so I asked if she could live with me. We have been together ever since. So, you see, family is not always blood, Roscoe."

"Thats what I say. I feel so bad for her never to have

that closer. I know that feeling."

"Yes, everyone has a story."

"So, what else is there to know about Newwart?" Roscoe asked Razor, trying to get more information without revealing his intentions. He remembered that Dr. Beal and Henry were also heading to Newwart.

"When you get a chance to go get their Reaver soup it's to die for as well, but enough about old stories and food for now. Back to work."

"It was just getting to the good stuff, Sgt!"

"Yeah, we need to focus back on the training, to the line. Ready, set go!" and Roscoe takes off again.

"Dr. Beal, we have arrived at Newwart," Randi says over the intercom.

Dr. Beal radios down to the Highyeah base. "Highyeah base, this is Dr. Brooklyn Beal on the

Federation space station 2625 requesting permission to land, over."

"We hear you, Dr. Beal." The base comms chief says over the radio. "You are clear to land. The emperor has sent a message for you as well."

"I'll take it when we land. I'll also need to speak to Chancellor Gann," Dr. Beal replies.

"Roger that, ma'am, he is at his estate in Hara," he responds.

The Federation station descends into Newwart, passing Mt. Tocan. The snow begins to fall, and they fly over the city of Hara as they make their way to the Highyeah Mt. base.

The station lands in the bay at the base of the Highyeah Mountains. As Dr. Beal exits the ship with Henry, she turns back to the maintenance crew and says, "The old girl has been through a lot. She's going to need some work."

"Yes, ma'am." They respond, walking in with their tools.

"Where can I hear the message from the Emperor, Commander?" she asks Commander Athena, who is waiting for them outside the ship.

"Up here," she says as she leads them to her office.

"Thank you," Dr. Beal says as Henry and she follow the Commander.

"You can hear it here." She opens her door and allows Dr. Beal to enter.

"Thank you. You two stay here, and I'll take it in private," Dr. Beal says.

Henry replies, "Me too?" feeling some way about it.

Dr. Beal replies, "Yes, you too. I'll keep you posted on any news."

Henry reluctantly settles, finding Dr. Beal very sketchy. He says, "OK."

Dr. Beal enters the office and notices a giant

portrait of Emperor Sophia Cascade behind the Commander's desk. She sits down in the Commander's chair, and as it spins around, a hologram of the emperor appears.

He says, "There have been attacks on food warehouses in Hara. Chancellor Gann needs our help. I need you to go down there and handle it. Figure out what is happening to the missing people."

She replies, "Yes, Emperor, I will take care of it."

He says, "We must handle this quietly and discreetly. The other Chancellors cannot find out, or it will cause more chaos, which will consume this galaxy."

Dr. Beal does not like the plan and says, "I think we should tell the Chancellors now, my Emperor."

He says, "No. this plan is what I feel is best for the people." He turns around, and the hologram disappears.

She leans back in the chair, closes her eyes, and takes a minute to think. Then, taking a deep breath, she runs her hands through her hair and sighs. "Okay, you two, you can come in now."

Henry enters first, sitting in a chair in the corner. The commander follows him, saying, "So what are the emperor's orders?"

She approaches them and says, "We need to head down to Hara. Four of your soldiers will accompany us."

Commander Athena looks at a pad. "Okay, Doc, I'll have someone meet you in the armory."

Henry jumps in and says, "What about those who attacked us? What are we going to do about them?"

Dr. Beal says, "They are gone now. We are fine." She quickly dismissed his statement so the Commander would not ask the question.

Noticing this, the Commander says, "Who were they?"

She says, "They are not what is important. They are gone now."

Henry, perplexed and angry by her response, says, "What are you talking about? They just tried to kill us."

She says, "We have orders from the emperor, and that is that. Now, Commander Athena, tell me about the food warehouse attacks."

Commander Athena replies, "They have been under attack for the last two weeks. As far as we can tell from all reports, it's just been some bandits."

"Ok," she says "We can handle that. I'll talk to Chancellor Gann and see if we can implement a curfew. He and my dad were old friends long ago. Maybe he will help. Now, what about the missing people? Are they dead or just missing?"

Still puzzled by her reports of missing people in Hara, the Commander says, "I have no idea about that."

Dr. Beal says, "We will investigate it when we arrive. We need some gear for the trip down."

Henry replies in shock, "What do you mean by on our way down?"

She says, "We have to use the snow Jeep speeders and camp halfway down because it will be nightfall when we arrive in the Darkhair Forest, and believe me, you don't want to be moving outside the pulse at night in there."

Henry says, "Then why don't we just take a Wing guider down." The Wing guider are choppers that look like birds with propellers on top of either wing and a tail that moves up and down.

Commander Athena replies, "Well, there is a storm rolling in, so the choppers are grounded."

They head to the armory to meet up with the four soldiers the commander gave them.

As they walk up, one of the soldiers asks Henry, "Blaster rifle or a pistol blaster?"

"What do I need a weapon for?" he says.

Dr. Beal replies, "We will be going through the Darkhair Forest. There are Reavers. They have been starving from what's been going on, so choose a weapon. This is real not one of your games. It's life or death. You must keep your guard and protect yourself where we are going, or things will get ugly quickly. Reavers are orange, black-striped, wiry-haired hounds that stand five feet tall with solid white eyes, so they can see very well at night and through the snow."

Henry shakes and says, "Oh my, okay. I have never shot a real one. Dang it. I'll take the big one, I guess."

Dr. Beal states, "We will head out to the Darkhair Forest in five minutes before it gets dark. Make sure we pack the tents and sensors for the perimeters. Once everything is loaded, we will roll out."

Dr. Beal, Henry, and the four imperial guards head to get on the snow speeders set up outside the motor pool.

Henry runs past Dr. Beal, "Can I drive?" he asks excitedly.

Dr. Beal laughs and replies, "Yes, sure." They all hop on and head down to Hara.

As soon as they leave, Commander Athena calls Chancellor Gann and says, "Chancellor, Dr. Beal, four imperial soldiers, and some kid are coming to see you, sir."

Chancellor Gann says, "Thank you, Commander,"

and hangs up.

Chapter 4

On Izeal, tension grows at the imperial palace, with people outside begging for food. Emperor Cascade is sitting in the dining hall, eating his evening soup.

His daughter Kelly Cascade storms into the dining hall, her long, black, curly hair bouncing with every step. She looks furious. Wearing her regular black and gold vest with a gold skirt equipped with a slot for her daggers that fit tight on her lean body, she places her daggers on the table and waves the servant over. "Father, my spies are telling me the Chancellors are having secret meetings about how we are handling things. Father, I fear the worst!" She pulls out her chair, sits, and starts to eat. With her mouth full of food she says, "The people are getting bolder. The food bank bombings on Newwart are just the beginning. Someone is stirring them up. It's probably that no good, Gann. The Chancellors are making a play for the throne, Father."

Emperor Cascade is sixty-three years old but looks tired and weary from everything that has happened over the years, and he has not been the same since his son's mysterious death some years back. His hand shakes as he takes a bite to eat, then says to her, "Oh my beautiful rose, your people are starving, and yet you are in here gorging on silver fox and fury meat."

She takes a bite, pulls the meat off the bone, and says, "They are only subjects, easily replaced. Perhaps we should send them to one of the lower cities?"

He shakes his head in disappointment and says, "That's why I sent Brooklyn to handle the situation on Newwart. You show no compassion for others."

She slams her fork into the table, and the guard step forward. The emperor raises his hand, and the guard steps back. "Father, how could you send your scientist to handle a military affair, which I thought was my job as your Admiral?"

He replies, "My dear, they are just scared and hungry

people. Sometimes, it's better to show compassion than steel." As he slowly gets up and walks down towards her, his bones creak together, making an awful grinding sound.

She turns her head and looks up at him. "How would you know? You rarely leave this palace? If we do not show them the steel, they will not stay in line. You put too much trust in those two. Why father?"

He pulls a chair out, sits beside her, grabs her hand, and says, "I have my reasons. Just trust me, this thing with the food will be over soon. The Chancellor's Summit will be in a couple of weeks, and we can talk to them then."

Angered by his decision, Kelly pulls her hand away, gets up, and says, "You are playing a dangerous game, father, and it will be the downfall of this family." She walks towards the door in the dining hall.

"My dear," he says, "We must stay the course. It's the best move I can see, right now."

Kelly mutters as she storms out of the dining room. "Fragile old man, I'll handle this myself." She reflects on how powerful her family once was and squeezes her fist.

"I'll rule like the Twins did. I promise this will not be our

legacy."

Back on the Dark Wolf, Roscoe enters the training

room and places one of the helmets on his head. He takes a

deep breath and begins the fighting sim. A dojo appears

and three armed men stand across from him. The buzzer

goes off and the first one charges him. He pulls out a knife

to stab Roscoe. Roscoe grabs the man's arm, stretching it

out, and turns around, breaking it over his shoulder and

causing the man to drop the knife. Roscoe picks up the

knife and then stabs the man in the stomach, making him

disappear. He rises to his feet and flexes, then gestures to

the next man to attack. The man pulls out two katanas and

charges at him. He roundhouse kicks the man in his face,

sending him flying, and crashing to the ground. He

approaches the man lying on the ground with the swords

next to him. Roscoe picks them up and stabs him in the chest. He runs at the next man and jumps into the air to double-knee him when he shadow-jumps and knees the man, knocking him out.

Roscoe stands up, looking himself up and down, confused by what he had just done. "*What the heck was that?*" *he thinks to himself.* He shakes it off and ends the sim. Roscoe removes his helmet as sweat pours down his head. He looks a lot different now than when he first arrived. His physique has changed dramatically, and he has built muscle in his abs and arms.

Lily enters the training room and sees Roscoe standing there with his shirt off. She does a double take, looking at his body up and down, and says, "Looks like the simulator is working. You look amazing, Roscoe."

Roscoe turns red and awkwardly says, "Thanks. I just wanted to pull my weight." He dries his head off, and they walk over to a workout bench and sit down.

Lily puts her hand on his and says, "Stop it, you are

not a burden. Also, thank you so much for coming to talk to me the other day. I needed it."

Looking at Lily and how amazing she is, Roscoe thinks. *Come on, Roscoe, get it together, don't mess this up.* "No problem. So, I have a question."

"What is it?"

"Have you always wanted to fly? I want to learn."

She feels a sense of pride. "Yes, it is an honor on Ma'de to join the Pilot Core. Luke and I joined when we were 17. We were the youngest to do it and made master faster than anyone from San-van. That's how we got assigned to the Dark Wolf.

After hearing this and being amazed by how much she had accomplished at such a young age, Roscoe becomes even more captivated by her. "Can you teach me to sail the stars and the oceans?"

She replied, "Yes, it would be my pleasure. We can visit some of Ma'de's underwater caves, where my brother and I played. They are divine this time of year! All the ocean gems light up the caves. It really is a sight to see!"

Feeling embarrassed, she said, "Sorry, I kind of geek out about sailing in general."

Roscoe's mood saddens as he replies, "No, no. It's ok. That sounds much better than Saint Ethel's. I used to sit on top of the roof, thinking about the stars, the wonders of the galaxy, and all the other worlds. So, I would love to see it, especially with you."

She grabs his hand and replies, "I can help you find out who your family is and where they are from if you like. " Her feelings for him grow with each conversation.

He can feel himself beginning to trust her more. "Thank you. Maybe, after all this is over, we can. Well, I want to hit the shower and take a nap before we get to Osiris. Randi, how much longer till we arrive at Osiris?"

Randi replies, "Tee minus two hours till arrival."

Roscoe gets excited. "Heck yeah, a hot shower is calling my name. I can also nap before we get there," slamming his fist into his hand. I'll see you later," he says to her.

As they stand up, he leans in to hug her. All excited, Lily thinks, "*Should I kiss him goodbye?*" Thinking he might want to kiss her too, she stumbles into his arms, tripping over her feet. She hugged him at the waist. They laugh out loud as he lifts her, kisses her forehead, and says, "Goodbye."

Feeling embarrassed, Lily looks down and away, saying, "Thanks for the catch and goodbye. See you later."

"Bye." Roscoe gets butterflies looking at her as he leaves.

He heads down the hall of the Dark Wolf. Thinking to himself how stunning and smart Lily is, he runs into Captain Mitchell, not paying attention.

Captain Mitchell says, "Keep your head up and out of the clouds, soldier."

He snaps to attention, letting Cap walk by as he enters the man's bathroom. He responds, "Yes, sir." He walks into one of the three empty showers, divided by brick walls as high as six feet on either side of the shower heads.

He says, "Randi, please turn the shower warm for me."

Randi responds, "Here you go, Roscoe," and the water turns on. He reaches into the water, pulls his hand back out, and shakes it off. "Just right. Thank you, Randi."

She says, "My pleasure."

"Hey Randi, can you turn on some music, please?" he asks while washing his hair.

Randi responds, "Yes, Roscoe. Your normal hits?"

"Yes, please," and music starts to play.

He enjoys his shower and gets out. He dries off and heads back to his room. As he gets to his room, he opens his door and heads to his locker in the corner. He grabs an Izealin black and gold combat uniform and puts it on. It's big and baggy on him, but he pulls the string hanging off the right wrist of the uniform, making it fit perfectly. The suit can read your vitals and control the temperature inside the uniform, among other things. It has full-outer space Capabilities for a time. However, the battery life and oxygen will expire after so long. Still exhausted from his workout earlier, Roscoe lies on his bed and falls asleep.

He opens his eyes, and once again, he is in the Dream Realm. Feeling confused about why he keeps coming here, he hears a voice again saying,

"This way to the truth, boy." He walks down the purple-smoked path toward the castle, thinking that's where the voice is coming from. He walks up to the castle's stairs and the front door. His hand trembles in fear, and he grabs the handle. Just as he opens the door, he is awakened by a loud noise that erupts in his head.

Captain Mitchell says, over the Dark Wolf's intercom, "Everyone, we have a briefing on the bridge in fifteen minutes. Over and out." Roscoe wipes the sweat from his head as his vitals race, his uniform warning him about his heart rate. He gets up, hits the override button on his jacket, and leaves his room, still shaken by the Dream realm.

Roscoe is trying to gain his bearings. As he walks

down the hall, holding his hand as it shakes. Oblivious to anything, he walks around the corner with his head down.

Luke runs right into him, walking and eating his apple.

Luke's apple hits the floor. "Come on, man, pay attention. What is wrong with you?"

Stumbling over his words, Roscoe says, "I-I'm sorry, man."

He looks at him and sees he is jittery. "Don't worry, man, it's all good. Are you good?" Slapping him on his back, they walk onto the bridge and over to the center computer.

Roscoe nods at him, "Ya, I'm good." As Lily enters the bridge, Roscoe sees her and waves,

"Hey, can I talk to you real quick?"

She replies, "Yes, what is it? Are you okay?"

As he is about to tell her about his dreams, Captain Mitchell walks in and says, "Roscoe, I got great news. Dr. Beal and Henry are all good. They are on-"

"Newwart," Roscoe says before Cap could finish his sentence.

Captain Mitchell and the rest of the team look at him sideways, and Captain Mitchell says, "How did you know that?"

Roscoe thinks to himself, *Holy shit, that was real* before saying, "Lucky guess?" *Was I Dream Weaving?*

Lily looks over at him, "Izeal to Roscoe. Are you ok?"

Roscoe says, "Yes, sorry, continue, sir."

Captain Mitchell says, "OK, team. As I said, we are looking for a smuggler named Tekey-Espy. He is known to spend much of his time at Meg's Piano Bar or the Track. We can get more information about the Track from Meg."

Razor says, "In the underground world, in Ojacka, Meg knows everything."

Captain Mitchell smirked and, looking over at Razor, "Yeah, she does, huh, Razor," hinting at the fact that they had a past. "When we get to Osiris, we will head down to

Ojacka to speak to Meg. Let's get our gear. Ophelia, get the kid a gun."

Ophelia and Roscoe head down to the armory on the ship to pick out a weapon for him.

As Roscoe leaves, Lily says, "Hey, Roscoe, you were going to tell me something?"

Roscoe looks back and replies, "It's ok. I'll just talk to you later," as he heads out.

Ophelia opens the armory door and walks in as Roscoe follows her. The wall flips over and there are pistol blasters, auto blasters, hammer-pistol blasters on one side, katana swords, and all other types of swords and daggers on the other. She holds her hand out to the room and says, "Pick your poison."

Roscoe picks up an auto blaster, holds it, feels the rifle's weight, and puts it down. Then he goes to the swords, picking up two and swirling them to his side. "I like these," he says as he slides them in the sleeves on his back. Then he reaches over and grabs a pistol, pointing it up in the air and looking down the sights. He holsters the pistol and says, "That will do."

Jeff standing behind him laughs and says, "Alright, young man. I see training has done you some good."

As Randi comes up on the intercom, she tells Captain Mitchell, "We are now entering the Osiris' rings, and I have navigated the safest path to Osiris," an asteroid belt that orbited Osiris.

He heads to the Dark Wolf's loading docks and says to her, "Roger that. Open coms so I can radio them on Ojacka."

She replies, "Yes, sir."

Captain Mitchell radios the post Samel, which is just outside the city of Ojacka. "This is Captain Mitchell of the Dark Wolf, asking for permission to land." He then enters the loading docks, where the rest of the team is getting their gear ready.

A soldier from the base says, "We read you, and you are clear to land."

Captain Mitchell grabs a black leather jacket with Cockapee fur and tells Randi, "OK, lower us down." He looks at Roscoe and says, "Keep your eyes peeled and tell no one about what Dr. Beal told you. We do not know who we can trust, where our enemies are, or who works with them."

As the Dark Wolf lowers into the landing slots on the post, Samel, the bay opens, grabbing the ship and locking it in place. Other drop ships are loaded into the holding yard. Chancellor Amri Graves walks out of the base control tower to greet them with four guards.

Captain Mitchell sees him approaching and tells Randi, "Lower the loading doors." The rest of the team grabs their Caps and other cold-weather gear.

Randi says, "Yes, sir."

As Captain Mitchell steps off Dark Wolf, he orders the team, "Offload the gear, Razor, you are with me. The rest of you meet us inside when you are finished. Also, Roscoe, remember what I said. Say nothing of what you are doing with us. " He looks back at him, holding his finger over his mouth.

Roscoe replies as he nods his head, "Yes, sir."

Captain Mitchell and Razor meet Chancellor Graves halfway between the Dark Wolf and the base.

Chancellor Graves is an average-sized man with long, black, slick-down hair to his shoulders. His olive skin makes the blue arrow across the bridge of his nose pop out. He approaches them with a group of soldiers wearing his traditional robes, which are white and red with Jackabe bird feathers on the shoulders. The Chancellor holds out his hand to shake Captain Mitchell's. "Good morning, Captain."

"Good morning, Chancellor. It's been a while since I have seen you."

"Yes, it has Captain." A woman walks up next to him. "This is Commander Way. She will give you whatever you need here in Samel."

She salutes Captain Michell and says, "It's an honor,

sir." They start to walk across the runway and make their way to the base.

She sees Razor and runs up to him, grabbing his hand and shaking it uncontrollably, "Sgt, your fight style, Suegin, is legendary here on Osiris. I practice it every morning. I wish I had been at the Academy when you were teaching."

"Alright, alright that's enough. Thank you." Razor pulls his hand away. "I have heard great things about you as well, Commander Way. You are on the shortlist to be the next Chancellor in waiting. That is a high honor from your people."

"Thank you so much, sergeant." She says in awe of him.

Jeff and Luke unload the ship, shaking from the cold. Luke spots Commander Way and says, "Oh my, will you look at her?"

Jeff says, "Yeah, right, you've got no chance," before pushing Luke out of the way to get to her first.

Luke shoves him back, and they scuffle back and forth, trying to get her attention.

Jeff trips Luke, who falls flat on his face. He runs up to her and says, "It is freezing here. Do you want to help keep me warm, Commander?"

Luke runs up behind Jeff and bumps into him. "Commander don't listen to the little one. Give me one night, and I will show you the stars for a lifetime," he says, kissing Commander Way's hand.

Ophelia shakes her head at them, shoves her way between them, and says, "You two are fools."

Commander Way pulls her hand away as Ophelia knocks Luke's grip loose. Weirded out by the situation, she awkwardly replies, "Um, no, thank you."

"You two get it together. You are soldiers in the emperor's army; show some respect," Razor scolds them.

Jeff and Luke pull it together, snap to attention, and say, "Yes, Sgt."

Chancellor Graves and Captain Mitchell continue to

talk as they walk towards the base. "It's been winter for more than six months. Our lakes are frozen over, and we can not harvest any fish. What is going on with the transport of fish? My people are starving."

Captain Mitchell holds the door open for him. "The emperor is taking care of it, sir."

Shaking his head, he says, "Oh, is he? Has he seen his people lately? The last time he was here was many years ago, my friend. When he loved his people and was not looking for traitors all around him, when was the last time he even left the Imperial City, Captain? Before Matthias's death?"

Razor strongly reminds Chancellor Graves. "Watch yourself Remember your place, and mind your words, Chancellor. That is your Emperor you're speaking about."

Chancellor Graves quickly changes his tone. "I mean no disrespect. I'm but a humble servant. What can I do to help? I am here to serve." Bowing to them.

Captain Mitchell replies, "It's okay, Chancellor. We

are all feeling the effects of the situation. We just need some speeders; that should be all."

Chancellor Graves says, "I can do that, but if you don't mind me asking, what are you doing here?"

They arrive at his office, and Captain Mitchell says, "Imperial business, that is it."

He shakes his head. "Yup, same old, same old secrets as always with him." As he enters his office on the base, "If you need anything else, do not hesitate to ask. I will be here till later. Commander Way will show you to your Jeep speeders. Now, good day, gentlemen."

As the rest of the team were making their way in, Captain Mitchell said, "Thank you."
Commander Way says, "Follow me this way," and leads them down a hall and into the motor pool. Two armored snow Jeep speeders, black four-doors with snow tracks for tires, were waiting for them. One big cannon blaster was coming out of the bowl shield turret.

Captain Mitchell raises a holographic map on his

wrist and says, "Link up." The rest of the team follow. "So, here's the plan: Razor, Luke, Roscoe, and I will be in the lead vehicle. The rest of you will take the other one and be the rear security. Keep your eyes peeled; our enemy can come from anywhere. Now load up."

The team responded, "Yes, sir."

Before they enter the speeders, Captain Mitchell tells Commander Way, "Thank you, and keep my ship on standby. We won't be here long."

"Yes, Captain." She salutes him and they drive out of the motor pool.

As they make their way down the snowy streets of Ojacka, Roscoe stretches his hand out of the window catching the snowflakes as they fall. Holding the cold, wet snow in his hand, he looks at Razor and says, "Wow, this is snow, huh? I have never seen it before. It's so cold, how did you live here?" He shakes the snow off his hands and then blows into them to warm them up.

Razor chuckles, "We are strong, resilient people,

unlike you inner planet-people. We Osirisins only know the cold." Luke slows down due to a line of speeders around the corner of an Ojacka food warehouse bank.

Captain Mitchell observes the situation and says, "Luke, just drive around them."

Luke pulls around the line and says, "Captain, look at this." Men, women, and children are in line with baskets, tubs, and crates for food for their families. Some people were so skinny that their clothes were hanging off their frail bodies. Their faces showed signs of deep-set hunger. "The people are starving, sir. We need to hurry."

Captain Mitchell, in anguish, says, "I know, I know." They pull up, and all get out. They head to the front door of a tall building. It had a red circle neon sign that read "Meg's Place." Razor opens the door and walks in first. You can't see anything down the hall, but a glimmer of red light at the end. The rest of the team enters behind him. They walk down the narrow hallway. You can hear soft music playing from the bar. Walking, they notice pictures of a woman playing the piano and many other bands on the walls. They reach the end of the hall, and a tall, pale woman with black hair and a piano key necklace around her neck approaches. She wore a skin-tight black dress with red shimmering stripes across her body. She had a blue arrow across her nose, like Razor.

She grabs Razor by the face and kisses him. "It has been a long time, my love."

Razor's face turns red. "I know, my dear."

Another woman walks up and leans up against the bar, staring at Ophelia, twirling her daggers around her fingers. "Hello, O."

Ophelia shakes her head. "Hello, Margo." Looking at her with disgust.

Margo is the half-sister of Chancellor Andrea Docain. Her mother is a Jaair, and her father is Lanardin. Like most Lanardins, Margo has fire-red hair, but like her mother, she refuses the Cockapee milk, which turns them yellow, so she has tan skin.

Margo smirks at her. "How long has it been? Since the Cleat Academy as initiates?"

Ophelia becomes angry. "Jaair, there's no need to bring up old stuff. You lost. Let it go."

Margo pulls her shirt down so they can see the scar on her chest. "Let it go? I will never! You embarrassed me in front of my father. I'm here and not an Imperial soldier because of you. He has not spoken to me since." She puts her right hand on her holster as if she were about to take her blaster out.

Ophelia puts her hands on her blaster. "You are lucky; that is all you have after what you pulled."

"You think you're still better than me? Call me Jaair again, and I'll show you some new things I've learned."

Ophelia laughs at her and says, "Same old Margo, blaming everyone and not taking responsibility for your actions. But I'll teach you again. If you like."

At this point, the two women are face to face, and Captain Mitchell says, "Alright. Alright! That's enough.

Let's get back to business, Meg. That's what you are right? A businesswoman." Margo and Ophelia back away but still stare at each other viciously.

Meg replies, "Why yes," in a very sly manner.

Trying to woo her over, Razor holds his arm out and says, "Come on Meg let's go to your office. We have some imperial business to discuss that would benefit you greatly."

She puts her hand on his arm and replies, "This way." They turn around and head towards a set of side stairs.

As she walks away, Roscoe notices that she has a red two-tailed Shoma tattooed on her back. The beautiful dragon is believed to guard the temples of the Creator.

Before he follows them, Captain Mitchell says, "Luke, Roscoe, and Jeff stay down here and keep your eyes out for Tekey-Espy." He leaves them and walks off, following Razor and Meg.

"Yes, sir," they say as each pulls a chair out to sit on at the bar.

Captain Mitchell looks back and says, "Don't get too comfortable, boys. Keep your senses clear."

Jeff laughs and looks at him, knowing he is talking to him. Then he says, "Yes, I'll just have one Cap, promise."

Captain Mitchell shakes his head and chuckles as he goes up the stairs with the others.

The bartender knocks on the bar before them and says, "So you want anything, honey?"

Jeff turns around and replies, "My dear, I'll take three shots of your best whiskey and you."

She blushes. "I don't think you can handle this," while pouring their shots.

"Come on, man, that's the best you got," Luke says, mucking Jeff as he sits next to Roscoe.

She looks at Luke and shoves his drink to him. "Shush."

Jeff laughs at Luke. He smiles back at her and says, "Thank you. You know what they say about the lovemaking of Rydeanians?"

Luke rolls his eyes, shakes his head at Jeff, and takes his shot—slamming his glass upside down.

She smiles and says, "No, what do they say?" She puts her elbows on the bar and places her head in her hands to listen to him closely.

He looks at her in her deep green eyes and says, "It's as fierce as the volcanoes on Mt. Kale and as deep as Ma'de's oceans."

She looks at him, bites her bottom lip, and says, "My shift ends in a few hours. If you want to return to my place, you can show me how fierce your lovemaking is, my little orange-haired man."

Jeff looks at his watch and sighs. "I would love to, but we are on a mission. The next time I'm in Ojacka, I'll look you up, my Ma'dein queen." He takes the shot.

As she pours them another shot, she says, "I'll hold you to that, my good sir."

Jeff holds up his shot, and the other two follow his lead. They say, "Here's to the ones we lost. May we meet in the stars.”

They smash their shots together, say, “May we meet in the stars,” and then drink them fast.

As the lights in the room begin to dim, a woman walks up on the stage, and the spotlight homes in on her. The music begins to play, and she starts singing a fantastic song.

Looking out the window above the bar at the stage in her office, Meg says, “So, what can I do for you?” She turns around and sits down in her chair behind her desk.

Captain Mitchell sits in the chair on the right, and Razor on the left. He crosses his legs and says, “We are looking for a smuggler named Tekey-Espy.”

Standing behind Meg, Margo says, “What do we get for this information?”

By the door, Ophelia says, “We can just make you. " Still revved up from their earlier spat, Margo steps towards her.

Meg raises her arm to stop her and responds,

"There's no need to make threats. We are all friends here, and I will give you what you need."

Razor says, "Thank you. Once everything returns to normal, we will ensure you are the first person the emperor sees about shipping the food to the other planets. For your time and information, Meg."

Meg, holding a fist full of coins, says, "See, now you're talking my language," as she drops coins into her hand. "He is at The Track. It's a barn just a mile outside Lake Nowell. They place bets on fury fights there."

"Thank you so much for the information, Meg," he says, then nods to Lily, and she throws her a bag of money.

Captain Mitchell stands up and says, "We have what we need. Let's move out."

As the team exits Meg's office, Margo says, "See you around, Ophelia," in a very devious voice.

Ophelia walks down the stairs, and says under her breath, "Not if I see you first, Margo," in a calm but vengeful tone.

Captain Mitchell and the rest of the crew return to the bar as the song ends, and all three guys have tears in their eyes.

Razor says to them, "Hey! Get your shit together, man."

Ophelia laughs at them as she walks by.

Jeff wipes his eyes off with his sleeve and says, "It was just dust."

Lily says, "There is nothing wrong with shading a tear to good music." She looks at Roscoe as she passes him.

Roscoe elbows Luke as he gets up from the bar, saying, "She feels the same about music." They all head out the front door.

Luke throws his hands up and replies, "I was not crying!" as he follows them.

As Roscoe enters the Jeep speeder, he looks across the street and notices a round, chubby, middle-aged man with short brown curly hair walking with a group of soldiers. The green crystal in the middle of his eyebrow caught his eye. "Hmm, I wonder who that is." Sitting in the back seat, Roscoe says, "Hey, Sgt, who is that over there with Chancellor Graves?"

Razor looks over his shoulder and out the back window, saying, "Oh, that is Chancellor London Cantrell from Tearocon. His family owns one of the largest harvesting farms on Tearocon. I wonder what he's doing all this way out here."

Captain Mitchell says, "It doesn't matter, stay focused and on task."

"Yes sir," they all say, and Roscoe turns around.

Chancellor Graves and Chancellor Cantrell enter the Blooming Flower Tea House as Margo watches them at the bar.

The waitress walks up to them with menus. "You want your normal table in the back, Chancellor?"

Chancellor Graves says, "Yes, and we'll have one more guest join us."

The waitress says, "Ok, this way, sir," as they follow her towards the back of the room. "Here you go. Would you like your normal, or do you need a menu?"

Chancellor Graves sits down with Chancellor Cantrell and says, "We will take a menu today. Thank you."

She passes out the menus. "OK then, I'll give you guys a minute to decide."

As she walks away, Chancellor Cantrell says, "She is pushing it on time. People can't see us all together for too long." He looks around the room, feeling nervous.

"Be calm, my friend. She will be here any minute. Find yourself a good lavender tea. It will calm your nerves."

Chancellor Cantrell chuckles and says, "Yeah, I'm calm, just a little treason and tea."

Chancellor Riley walks up to the table and removes her hood. "Hey, you want to be a little louder and get us all killed?"

Pulling his monocle out of his jacket and looking at the menu. "No, I like my head, sorry."

Chancellor Graves waves to the waitress and says, "No one is dying if we do this right. Hold on."

As she walks up, he says "We will take the Jade delight, please."

She grabs their menus. "Good pick, sir. I'll put that in for you."

As she turns and walks away, Chancellor Riley says, "Can we trust our words here?"

Chancellor Graves nods. "We are good. She is very discreet in this manner and keeps me informed about things that go on around Ojacka."

Chancellor Cantrell says, "Okay, let us get on with this then. We all know the emperor is getting old, and we do not want another age like the Twins. We cannot allow Kelly to succeed to the throne. She would be a tyrant like them, taking what little power, we have now and pushing us out, or worse."

Chancellor Riley looks at him, puzzled. "This is not about our power. It's about our people's survival."

"We are the people's power," he tells her while the waitress walks up with their tea and three cups.

Chancellor Graves says, "Calm down, you two. We are all here for what's best for our people." The waitress places the teapot and tea on the table.

He says to her, "Thank you,"

She replies, "You're welcome. If you need anything, just let me know."

Chancellor Cantrell waits for her to leave and says, "Not all of us will agree with our decision. What do we do with Andrea Docain? You know her family and the royal family are close."

Chancellor Riley grabs the teapot and pours some into each of their cups. "We are not talking about removing any Chancellor yet."

Chancellor Cantrell grabs his tea and smells it. "Hmm, so we are good with rebellion but not murder."

She answers, "Yes, but we do not all need to resort to violence to accomplish our mission."

Chancellor Cantrell takes a drink and says, "Just wait, Jocelyn. Before this is over, you too will have blood on your hands."

Chancellor Graves picks up his cup and says, "Calm down, you two, and let us enjoy this cup of good tea. We don't know when it will be our last." They all take a sip. "London, we will continue with the proposed plan. If Andrea becomes a problem, then and only then will we deal with it. Agreed?"

They both say, "Agreed."

Just before he drinks, he says, "Here is to our friends and families that we've lost. May we meet in the stars."

They salute and repeat, "May we meet in the stars."

Margo watches them in front of the tea shop but cannot hear what they are saying, so she eventually gets up and leaves. She gets a call as she walks down the snowy streets of Ojacka.

She answers the phone. "They were all there like you said. What would you like for me to do?"

A woman's voice on the other end says, "Follow Cantrell and keep an eye on him for now. I'll get hold of you again."

Margo walks towards Meg's and replies, "OK, I'll stay with Chancellor Cantrell. " She hangs up and heads back to Meg's. She walks across the snowy street, looking for Chancellor Cantrell, who is still in the tea shop.

Jezdeal monks from the Church of the Creator step in front of her, not allowing her to pass. The sun shines on their shaved, bald heads, which they do to resemble the Creator. They wear golden robes, sandals, and chains with a talisman engraved with a C.
"Move aside, you motherless dog Jaair. We are walking here." The others spit at her feet, showing their disdain for her race.

Margo starts to pull out one of her throwing knives but stops herself. "We are not on Lanard. I would move aside, monks, if you know what is best for you."

They step aside, and their leader says under his

breath, "Our way will be everywhere soon enough. Your family protects you from us for now, Margo Docain," as she walks back into Meg's.

She returns to the bar; Meg sees her wipe the tears from her face. She gets up from playing the piano to check on her. Walking up to the bar where Margo is standing, Meg shouts to the bartender, "Two shots for my girl and me!"

The bartender reaches behind the bar, grabs a bottle and two glasses, and replies, "Yes, ma'am coming right up."

"Thank you," she answered, "So what did they say this time?"

"It does not matter. Nothing I have not heard my whole life," Margo replies as the bartender pours their shots.

"Very well, just know this is not Lanard. We may believe in the Creator like them, but we all don't believe like them," Meg states.

"Thank you, my friend," she replies as they cheer.

Meg nods, says, "Anytime," and cheers her back.

"May we meet in the stars," they say, then toast before chugging down their shots.

One of Margo's men enters Meg's and informs her that Chancellor Cantrell is leaving.

Margo places her glass on the bar. "Well, back to work," she sighs. "I'll come back when I can.

The team drives pass the frozen Lake Nowell, Roscoe looks out his window as the snow falls on the ice, with the giant trees surrounding it, where the great Jackabe lives.

Roscoe says to Razor, "You have such a beautiful home."

Looking at the peaceful view as the daylight begins to pierce through the clouds, Razor says, "Yes, I do." With a look of peace, he adds, "I remember getting up early with my dad and going to hunt snow stags."

Roscoe excitedly says, "Snow stags are such majestic creatures. That's so awesome you guys got to see one. Was it male or female?" Roscoe was very intrigued.

Razor chuckles at him. "Yes, for real. Calm down, I'll tell you a story. It was an early morning, just as the sun was rising. I believe Ophelia was about twelve at the time. I was taking her out to learn to hunt where my father took me. Her infrared had just started to develop, which happens to all Newwart women at that age. She and I had just reached the tree line as the sun pierced through the forest. We saw the snow move in a clearing, and a stag stood. She just stood up and shook the snow off her. It was a beautiful albino female."

"Oh, my Creator, how I wish I could have been there."

Razor shakes his head and continues. "I looked over at Ophelia, and a crazy thing happened, that stag and her locked eyes. It was as if they saw something so pure in each other at that moment it was beautiful. I didn't see a twig and stepped on it. It looked back at me, and it just walked off. I never got the honor to see another since."

In utter disbelief, Roscoe says, "Wow, what I would give just to see one."

"We are here. Game faces on," Captain Mitchell says as the Jeep speeders approach a massive metal barn with balconies on both sides. Two armed thugs walk alongside, watching what is going on inside through the open windows. There is also an armed thug and a camera at the front door.

Captain Mitchell grabs the radio. "Remember, from all the information we have gathered, this place is run by the Thug Lord, Jabari. He runs guns, Fury fights, and drugs. Jeff, I want you up in one of those trees to get a good viewpoint of the top floor. The rest of you are with me. Keep your eyes peeled. He'll do anything to keep what's his."

They all say, "Yes sir!" as they all get out, grab their gear, and head to the front door of the Track. Jeff runs to the nearest tree, ducking behind other Jeep speeders and

snow vehicles.

Jeff makes it to the tree, looking up, "Shit Cap, you

owe me for this one. This tree is tall!"

As the rest of the team approached the front door,

Captain Mitchell said, "I got you. Beers on me tonight.

Now let's get this done."

The guard at the front door holds them up. "What

can I do for you guys?"

Captain Mitchell says, "We are here on imperial

business. Now tell your boss to let us in."

The thug looks up at the camera, puts his finger on

his ear, and then looks back. "Ok, you can go in," he says

as the doors of the Track open.

The team enters and sees three rings in front of

them: one to the right, one in the center, and one to the

left. Above each one is an ample, oversized pendant light

hanging from the rafters. Crowds surround each of the

rings, screaming for their fury to win. There are side rooms draped in red and white silk doors. Tables of people are inhaling red dust. In the back of the room is a cashier's cage with an office on top with a large window that overlooks everything.

"Okay, Roscoe, let's see if your training pays off. How many armed men do you see around the room," Razor asks.

He scans the room. "Okay, Sgt., I spot two up top, one covering the side door, the three doing a figure eight-point rotation around all three rings, always keeping an eye on them. I also spotted one on the back wall with his blaster under his suit. I'm guessing he is the boss's bodyguard."

Captain Mitchell nods his head. "Hell, great eye, kid."

He replies, "Thanks, sir." He nods his head at Cap.

Captain Mitchell says, "Ophelia and Luke, you guys take the left side; Roscoe and Lily, you take the middle, and we'll take the right. You guys keep your eyes open and watch each other's backs. We need to find Tekey-Espy and get the hell outta here."

"Yes, sir," the team heads into the crowd of people.

As they move through the large number of people, Luke and Ophelia push them to the side to reach their ring.

Luke tells her, "Look at these people just giving up and wasting their money on nothing. Is this who we are trying to save?" He looks around at the people snorting the red dust in disgust. "Fools would rather starve than not get high, what a disgrace."

Ophelia says, "Come on, Luke, cut them a break. We are all going through a hard time. These people are lost and do not know what to do. It's just their way of coping with their situation." They need our help."

Luke says, "Sure," They walk up to their ring.

Not seeing him, Ophelia says to Cap, "he is not over here, sir."

Captain Mitchell pushes through the crowd. "We are almost to our ring. Just head over to the middle ring."

"Yes, sir," they say in unison.

Captain Mitchell and Razor move closer to the front of their ring. "Different day, same thing. We are getting too old for this, my friend," Captain Mitchell says.

Razor laughs and replies, "I know you are getting old, " as they approach their ring.

Captain Mitchell smirked, looking around, and said, "Nothing here either. Where is this guy?"

Razor looks around the room. "Roscoe and Lily, what about you guys? Any luck?"

"This place is crowded. We could barely move through here, but we're getting close now," Lily says.

Roscoe leans to the side and notices a man who fits the description of Tekey-Espy. He points to a man just a few people ahead of him, nudging her. "Hey, Lily, I think that's him."

She looks at him and nods. "Cap, I think we got eyes on him."

Captain Mitchell turns towards their direction, "Ok,

everyone moves in on their location."

As the rest of the team approaches, Roscoe says, "He is right over there pointing to the man wearing a green vest with curly brown and silver matted hair.

The team approaches him as he takes a big drink from his round flask. Tekey-Espy burps and stumbles into the guy next to him.

The guy yells, "Watch where you are going, Rydeanian!"

Tekey-Espy glances over to his vast hammer-ax, which is the same size as him. Standing on the floor beside him, he hiccups. "You hear that, Tearocon, Delilah? Should I show him your ass end?"

The man puts his hand on his holster, "Stupid little man, I'll kill you where you stand."

Captain Mitchell steps between the two and says, "Not today, Friend. Carry on now."

The man stars Tekey-Espy down, yelling, "Next time, you won't be so lucky when your friends are not around."

Tekey-Espy hiccups and says, "You're the lucky one, boy. This young man stepped in your way, or your Tearocon brains would be all over the floor!" yelling at the man.

Looking down at Tekey-Espy, Captain Mitchell says, "Sir, we need to talk to you. It is imperative."

Tekey-Espy takes another drink from his flask and replies, "I'm busy, boys. Come back later." He turns back to the rings and continues watching the fights.

Luke grabs Tekey-Espy by the arm and yells, "Listen, here we are on imperial business, and you need to answer our questions!"

Tekey-Espy hiccups and says, "Delilah, if this boy touches me again, I'm going to put your face through his skull," he slurs.

Luke grabs his sword and yells, "Who are you talking to, drunken old fool."

Tekey-Espy takes another drink, "My Hammer-ax,

would you like to get acquainted with her?" Everyone looks

at his Hammer-ax.

Captain Mitchell says, "Calm down, Luke. We have

no time for this." He looks down at Tekey-Espy and says,

"Sir, we are just here for the power core. Where is it?"

Tekey-Espy hiccups and laughs, "That's the darndest

thing, boys. Ya just missed it. I give it up for a bet on this

next Fury fight."

Razor, irritated, says, "Are you freaking kidding me,

to who?"

Tekey-Espy points his finger to the office above the

cashier's cage and says, "Him."

Captain Mitchell looks at him and says, "Ok, you are

coming with us then."

Tekey-Espy tips his flask over, "Will there be

whiskey?"

Luke says, "Just come on," pushing him along. The

rest of the team follows behind them, watching for

something to happen.

As they come to the back of the Track, the guard says, "What can I do for you, gentlemen….and ladies?" He signals over three more thugs.

Captain Mitchell shakes his head and says, "We are not here for what you guys are doing today. You all get a pass. We just need a word with your boss."

The guard looks around and says, "Ok, this way, only the three of you and the drunk," pointing at Captain Mitchell, Razor, and Roscoe, "That's all."

Captain Mitchell points at Tekey-espy. "He is coming too."

"Fine," The guard replies and then walks up the stairs.

Captain Mitchell leans toward Luke and says, "I don't like this. Be ready. " Then, he, Roscoe, and Tekey-Espy head up the stairs to Jabri's office.

As they reach the top, the guard leans in, knocks on the door, and says, "Hey boss, some imperial soldiers are out here. They want to talk to you."

A voice from the other side of the door says, "OK, come in."

They enter the room, the guard first, then Roscoe, Razor, Tekey-Espy, Captain Mitchell, and the three thugs follow behind them. When they enter the room, they see a broad-shouldered man towering over everyone with long black hair in a ponytail and dark brown eyes. His face is badly scarred, but you can still see some of the blue arrow that went across his face. He wore a dark blue shinny suit that matched his shoes and a gold chain.

He stands up and says, "Master Razor, I heard you were on Osiris. Men, it's an honor. I hear you are very skilled at Suegin, and your dojo was once second to none." Don't get me started on the thousands of men and women you chopped down in the Newwart Rebellion. You are a legend. Maybe we can go a few rounds," he throws punches in the air.

Razor says, "Thanks, but I'm not that man anymore."

Captain Mitchell cuts Jabri off just as he is about to say something else. "Enough with the groveling. We have no time. We need the power core this Rydeanin gave you."

Jabri sits back down in his chair. It almost touches the floor, considering how big he is. He leans back, rocking and cracking his peanuts, and replies, "This drunken fool gave it to me for a bet, so it's mine."

Tekey-Espy, offended, hiccups and asks, "Delilah, you hear this ogre? It seems to me this child needs a lesson in manners."

Jabri slams his fist on the desk, and peanut shells go everywhere. "Manners, you come into my place and want to talk about manners?" He is consumed with rage, points, and yells, "Kill these fools and start with the drunken one first!"

Captain Mitchell shakes his head and says, "Wrong move." Jabri's men unsheathe their swords and remove their blasters.

Captain Mitchell stands up, flips the chair in front of

him, and orders, "Ok, Jeff, now!"

Two shots go off, and the two guards walking on the balcony crash through the window.

Razor tells Roscoe, "Show them what it means to go up against the emperor."

Roscoe unsheathes his swords, takes out his pistol blaster, and whispers, "Yes, Sgt." in the blink of an eye, Roscoe and Razor begin to tear through Jabri's men, cutting their limbs off left and right.

Legs, arms, and a head go flying. Blood splats on the window overlooking the rings, orange-blaster fire and smoke fill the room, and the thug's head lands on Jabri's lap. Razor kicks the headless thug out of the window. A thug on the ground level charges at Ophelia, and she fires her blaster, piercing the man's skull and burning it all the way through. The thug begins to fall, as she stares through the hole in his head. Lily shoots out her grappling claw, grabbing a thug who is about to stab Ophelia in the back, pulling him towards her. Then she shoots him in the face before jumping on top of him, stabbing him over and over again, spilling blood all over her face.

Luke yells "Lily." She is so bloodlust that she does not hear him nor notice the woman about to shoot her. Luke throws his knife into her chest just in time.

All the firing stops, and Captain Mitchell walks up to Jabri, sitting behind his desk, and says, "You can give us what we came for, be collared and spend five years on the Istation or die here and now." The Istation is a hundred-foot column with pods around each column that orbits just above Izeal. The prisoners in the pods wear helmets like in the training room, but it repeatedly shows their worst fears.

Jabri looks up at him and reaches for his blaster. "I'm never going back to that hell."

Cap steps on it before he could reach it. "We could have handled this very differently, and now you are going to die on this cold, dirty ground. Pointless." He points his blaster at his head and shoots, and Jabri falls over.

Looking around at all the carnage as blood drips

down walls, Tekey-Espy says, "Delilah, they are just as crazy as we are. Where do we join?"

Captain Mitchell says, "You want to help? We need a builder. Your people were once known for your forging. Do you know of one?" as he picks through Jabri's pockets, looking for the core.

Tekey-Espy scratches his head and says, "I have heard of one. He goes by the name Dorn James. He lives outside Bearsekk in a cave just west of the Red Waste."

Cap looks around and radios, "All clear?"

"We are good down here, Cap," Ophelia replies as they check the dead bodies.

"Guys, we are looking for a safe. He would have never trusted anyone with it." Cap says to Razor and Roscoe.

Razor and Roscoe check through everything, and Razor says to Roscoe, "Not too bad for your first fight."

Roscoe looks behind a picture on the wall and replies, "Thanks, Sgt, it was nothing like I thought it would be. They were easy to beat."

Razor flips the rug, saying, "They were some paid muscles with little training. It won't always be that easy."

He looks behind a shelf on the wall, which reveals a safe. He says, "Hey, sir, I think I found it."

Captain examines the safe and says, "Yes, but we need some explosives, Ophelia?"

Cleaning blood off her boots, Ophelia replies, "Yes sir?"

Captain Mitchell grabs a chair and moves it away from the safe, giving them more room. He says, "We will need some explosives for this. Ophelia, go get the TNT from the Jeep speeder."

Ophelia starts to run outside and answers, "Yes, sir."

When she gets to the Jeep speeders, Jeff leans against one, smoking a cigar. He asks, "What's going on? Is it not over?"

She rubs her hands together and replies, "Yes, just need some explosive to blow some shit up and we should be good after."

Jeff takes a drag and says, "Good, no need for me,"
as he smokes his cigar, making smoke rings.

Ophelia opens the back of the Jeep speeder, grabs
their explosives, and heads back upstairs.

When she gets back, she says, "Got it, Captain."
They set the charge, blow open the safe, and grab the core.

Captain Mitchell puts it in his pack, turns, looks at
Tekey-Espy, and says, "OK, sir. Do you have a ship?"

Tekey-Espy laughs and says, "Batha is the fastest
gen-one on this side of the galaxies." They were small ships
used during Drew's conquest.

As the team heads outside the Track, Captain
Mitchell says, "Okay, good. We need to go to Newwart first
to get the rest of our team, and then we will meet you in
Bearsekk in ten days."

Tekey-Espy gets on his snow bike and heads toward
Ojacka.

Looking up that way, Captain Mitchell says, "Ok, guys, load

up. Those clouds look like they could get nasty, so we should get off this rock before it does."

Luke walks over to Jeff, looking concerned as everyone is loading up. "Jeff, hey man, can you switch me speeders? I need to talk to my sister."

Jeff says, "Everything good, man?"

Luke shrugs his shoulders and says, "I don't know if she can't shake what happened to our father; she went straight up bloodthirsty and lost focus and almost got shot."

Jeff, showing concern for his friend, says, "Sure, man, go ahead."

After putting his equipment in the back, Roscoe stops Lily as she walks by and asks, "Are you okay? " He then grabs her hand, noticing the rage on her face.

She says, "I'm fine, don't worry about me." as she wipes blood off her hand and walks away. Roscoe, worried about her, gives her a look but continues to finish loading up the equipment.

As the team takes off, Lily looks in the back seat and asks Luke, "What the heck are you doing here?"

Luke says, "I needed to talk to you. What was that shit back there at the Track? That was not like you."

Lily side-eyes him and says, "You are worried about me. Maybe you should look at yourself. You lost it on Tekey-Espy earlier, and I said nothing. Also, don't think I don't see you every night in the sim. What are you doing?"

Ophelia grabs her hand and says, "Calm down. He is only trying to help you. You lost your focus back there."

"Did I not save you? Real loss of focus huh?"

Luke says, "We are trying to help. At least I'm trying to deal with it. You are not, and if you don't, you are going to get yourself or someone else killed."

As the snowfall increases, a drop-ship descends from the clouds above and fires at them.

Captain Mitchell radios the post, "Hey, this is Captain Mitchell. Do you read me?" Evading the blasts.

The Samel radio chief says, "We read you; it's a bit

spotty, but we hear you. What's going on?"

Captain Mitchell says, "A drop-ship is firing upon us. How did you not see them?"

The radio chief, trying to get the radio to work, says, "Captain, we are having trouble with the system. It must be this storm."

Captain Mitchell gets on comms and says, "We are on our own. Start evasive movements, Ophelia, and head for the tree lines.

Roscoe looks out the window and sees the Falcon20 on the side. He remembers his dream and screams, "That's her. We got to go, Cap."

"How do you know who that is, kid?" Jeff asks as the Jeep speeder swerves back and forth.

"I just do. Hurry!" Knowing she is coming for him.

As they get closer to the tree line, the drop ship fires and hits the last Jeep speeder with Lily, Luke, and Ophelia. They land on the ice. It breaks, and the Jeep speeder descends into the cold, dark lake as the drop-ship zooms off.

Roscoe yells, "Lily! Stop the speeder, Jeff! Now!"

As the Jeep speeder comes to a stop, Roscoe jumps out and runs toward where the other went into the ice. He feels that tingling feeling all over again. Roscoe disappears into a cloud of blue smoke and reappears, where the Jeep speeder falls through the ice.

Razor and Jeff look at each other in utter disbelief, and Jeff says, "What was that?"

Razor shakes his head. "I don't know. It looks like what she does but blue."

Roscoe presses a button on the right side of his chest, and his suit heats up. He then dives in and swims down to the Jeep Speeder as it descends into the dark blue lake. When he reaches the Jeep Speeder, he sees Luke unconscious in the back. It's taking on water quickly.

Lily says, "Roscoe, get Luke out of here! He is hurt." Roscoe cuts Luke out of the back seat and brings him back to the surface as Razor dives in. He gets to the Jeep speeder, opens the driver-side door, pulls Ophelia out, and swims her back to the surface. On his way up, he sees Roscoe swimming back down to the Jeep speeder, sinking into the cold, dark water with no light.

As Razor gets to the top and pushes Ophelia out of the water, Jeff and Cap arrive and take care of Luke and her. Razor, shaking, says, "I don't know if they will make it, Cap." Where is Roscoe and Lily?" Cap asks, looking around for them.

Razor looks into the hole in the ice as the others do. "Down there."

"Come on, kid, you got this," Jeff whispers as they stand on the frozen lake.

Out of nowhere, Roscoe's suit begins to fail because of the extreme cold. He starts to freeze, but his body begins to glow. A blue aura surrounds him, lighting up the darkness and keeping his body warm. When he gets to the Jeep speeder, Lily is unconscious, so he swims into it, grabbing her tightly and swimming towards the surface.

The rest of the team sees the bright blue light shining in the darkness as he rises to the top of the frozen lake.

When he reaches the surface, he says," She needs help now," pushing her from the icy water.

The team looks at Roscoe in shock. As he emerges from the water, his blue aura disappears, and Captain Mitchell says, "We need to get them to the drop-ship now. We will talk about this later."

The team returns to the drop ship and rushes Lily to the medical bay, where they put her in the medical pod. Captain Mitchell then asks Randi, "What's the diagnosis?"

Randi says, "She has severe hypothermia; she should be dead. We must keep her body heated, and she will need rest."

Captain Mitchell says, "You heard her. There is nothing more we can do. Randi set a course for Newwart. She should be good by the time we get there, right?"

"Yes, Captain."

"Good, the rest of you get some sleep."

Roscoe pulls a chair beside the tube and says, "I'm staying here with her." Captain Mitchell puts his hand on Roscoe's shoulder and says, "She will be ok. She is one tough S.O.B.," and he leaves

Chapter 5

Back on Newwart Dr. Beal, Henry, and the group of soldiers enter the Darkhair forest. As the moon rises and peeks over the Highyeah mountains, Dr. Beal radios the group to stop. "It's getting dark. We need to make camp. We do not want to encounter a group of Reavers in the open. Reports have them hunting more south than normal."

Glancing around in a panic, Henry says, "So how do you plan on keeping them from coming into camp, if you don't mind me asking?"

A tall woman with dark brown hair approaches them. She was one of the imperial soldiers who came with them. "Don't worry. I got you, sweet thing. I won't let them hurt you." Slapping Henry on the butt.

Dr. Beal laughs. "Henry don't worry. I have some Tampers to go around the camp, and they will give off a pulse that keeps the Reavers away."

Thrilled to hear this, Henry says, "So, can we please make the Sosa Tubs in the protected zone? Roscoe and I have always wanted to try them."

Dr. Beal throws Henry the Tampers. "I don't see why not, seeing how you are the one who will be setting them up. You will need to turn it to the right and then push the top button, and then it's set. Make sure you do that before putting them in the ground."

As he juggles the Tampers, he is shocked by what she tells him. "By myself?"

Dr. Beal bends over and pulls the tents out of the packs. "Yes, everyone has a job."

He doesn't like it, but before he runs off, he says, "OK, then. I'll go!"

She chuckles. "There you go. Everything will be okay. Just keep your weapon with you and your eyes up."

The soldier walks up. "I got my stuff done. I'll go with you." Her eyes begin to glow red.

Henry says as they walk through the snow, "So where are you from?" He kneels to set the first Tamper.

She looks around checking for Reavers. "My family is from this little fur trade town called Wellbright, but we moved to Hara because some doctor's experiment got the town closed down."

They walked down about a yard and plugged the next Tamper into the ground, Henry replied, "Oh man, I am sorry."

"It's all good, how many more Tampers do you have left?" She is ready to get in the Tubs.

His hands tremble from the cold. "One more left if you want to go back and get ready. I got this."

She looks at him, questioning whether she should leave him or not. "Are you sure?"

Henry walks to place the last one. "Yes, I got this. I'll see you in the Tubs."

She was hesitant to leave him. "Okay, are you sure?

Henry stops, looks back at her, and shows her the

blaster. "Yes, I got this."

She looks around and doesn't see any Reavers. "Okay, just make sure you set it right."

"I will go on ahead." He waves her on, and she runs back to camp.

Henry is getting the last Tamper ready when he hears music start to play at the Tubs. He gets excited and forgets to press the top of the Tamper down before placing it into the ground, then he runs off.

As Henry passes the Tubs, she says, "You better hurry; it's nice and warm here."

Henry hears this, gets more excited, and takes his jacket off. When he arrives at the camp, he sees three double-wide, gold and black tents set up around a fire.

He says, "Dr. Beal, are you not going to come enjoy the hot waters? It was a long ride."

Sitting in a chair around the fire, Dr. Beal looks up from her book. "No, I'm just going to hang back and enjoy this." She picks up the book and shows him.

Henry says, "Oh, I am sorry, I didn't mean to disturb you."

She replies, "It's fine."

Henry points at the tents. "Which one is mine?"

Dr. Beal points at the middle one. Henry changes into shorts, a robe, and snow boots.

Dr. Beal stops Henry before he leaves. "You made sure that all the Tampers were set, right?"

Grabbing a towel, Henry says, "Yes, I did," as he runs towards the tubs.

He gets there, and the three guys are in one, and the female soldier is in the other by herself, and she waves him over. "Hey, you want to join me?"

Without hesitation, Henry removes his robe and boots. "Hell yeah," and jumps in.

She slides into the water up to her shoulders and looks up at the stars. "So, how are you liking my home so far?"

Henry is doing the same, just across from her. "A little too much snow for my blood if you ask me."

"Where I am from, this time of the year, it's summer. The trees and forest are so beautiful right now. But summer here is just amazing, and the tubs are divine."

"I need to come back then, I guess."

"Yeah. Come closer. I won't bite." She waves him over.

Henry begins to move over to her side of the tub when a Reaver comes from out of the shadows and sinks its teeth into her shoulder, dragging her out of the tub and into the dark as she screams for help from Henry. Henry was utterly frozen in horror and could not move. The soldiers in the other tub next to him scream in horror. "Reavers!" They all jump out of the tub and run toward the camp to get their blasters.

Henry is still frozen in the tub as he hears the woman screaming and being ripped apart in the dark, unaware of another Reaver sneaking up behind him.

Dr. Beal yells, "Henry, get down!" As the Reaver lunges towards him, she fires upon it, hitting the Reaver and knocking it down. She waves at Henry and yells, "Get out now! Let's go!"

Henry finally hears her and snaps back. He hops out of the tub and runs towards Dr. Beal.

Henry gets to camp, shivering and with blood all over him, crying. "I think it's her blood." He passes out as blaster fire goes off all around him.

Henry hears Dr. Beal say, "There is one over there!" as his eyes close.

Henry awakes, and Dr. Beal and only one imperial soldier are left.

"What happened?" he asks as he rises to his feet.

Dr. Beal wipes orange blood off her with a cloth and says, "Come here, you might want to sit down for this."

"Just tell me."

"Okay, we checked the Tampers, and you did not set one of them right."

Henry dropped to his knees and broke down. "Oh no, what have I done? I'm so sorry."

The imperial soldier covers up the two dead soldiers and says, "May we meet in the stars."

Dr. Beal helps Henry to his feet and brings him to a chair. She sits down in the one next to him, and he lays his head on her shoulder.

"We all make mistakes, Henry. I have made one that I believe may cost us dearly, if I don't fix it."

Henry sobs on her shoulder as the smoke from the fire smothers, he whispers. "I feel not as grave as mine."

She rubs the blood off his head and says, "I lied to you and Roscoe when we first met. I know who that woman is to him."

He lifts his head from her shoulder. "What do you mean? Why would you not just tell us the truth when we arrived?"

"I made a call. We don't know what she wants with him, so I didn't want him to go searching for her."

Henry is curious. "Why would he go searching for her?"

Dr. Beal takes a breath and looks away. "Cause she's, his mother."

"How could you keep that from him?" Henry says tears in his eyes.

"I made a choice that I thought was best at the time, and I'll have to deal with that. I believe how you deal with a mistake is the real test of a person. So, I am trying to atone for this mistake, starting with you and telling you the truth. What will you do?"

Henry goes to his tent. "I don't know. Family is a very important way to figure out who you are, and you kept that from him. I guess we both will have to deal with choice we made."

She starts to clean the blood off her hand. "Henry, everything will be ok I promise. Get some sleep. We will be in Hara by midday tomorrow."

Meanwhile, on the Dark Wolf, the monitor beeps as the medical tube opens, and Lily awakens. She looks over at Roscoe, who is sleeping in the chair next to her. "Hi, have you been here the whole time?"

Roscoe stands up and stretches. "Yes. Do you need anything?"

Lily sits up and coughs. "Some water, please."

He walks over to the faucet and pours her water. "Hey Randi, how are her vitals looking?"

He walks back and Randi answers, "By all my calculations, she is clear to do all physical activities."

Roscoe hands her the water and says, "I'm so glad you are okay."

"Thank you," Lily says as she takes a drink.

Roscoe sits back down, still stretching his body.

"No problem."

She clears her throat and asks, "So, how are Ophelia

and my brother?"

He reached over, grabbed her hand, and said, "Don't worry; everyone is well. They are just worried for you."

She takes another drink. "Thank you, by the way, for saving us."

Roscoe stands up. "Lily, there is no need to thank me. I care about you a lot." Would you like for me to get you more water?"

Lily hands him back the cup and says, "Yes, please." She sits up in the tube and gets out.

Roscoe grabs the cup and walks over to the faucet to get her more. "So, do you remember anything?"

"Just a blue light."

It's just like on Ma'de Roscoe thinks to himself as he turns around to bring her the water, he sees her bent over, and her butt is showing. He turns back around trying to be respectful. "I'm so sorry, the back of your gown is open."

She walks over to Roscoe, who has his back to her, grabs his hand, and he turns around. "Don't worry about what happened down there. I am alive because of you. We are all here because of you, so thank you," she kisses him.

He kisses her back and says, "I love you, Lily." They continue to kiss as he caresses her back.

She grabs his hand and a blanket from the rack as they walk over to the front of the medical tube. They lay the blanket down and lie on it, and he begins to rub his fingers through her hair while he kisses her, thinking of how beautiful she is.

While kissing him, she climbs on top of him, wrapping her legs around his waist. She takes his shirt off, rubbing her hand on his chest, feeling his heartbeat. She kisses his neck and whispers, "Oh, Roscoe, I love you too."

They pull their clothes off and begin to make love.

As Roscoe sleeps, Lily watches him and rubs his head. "Hey, Randi, Dim the lights, please."

"Yes, Lily."

Lily lies her head on his chest and falls asleep.

Chapter 6

Roscoe opens his eyes, and he is on Ma'de. He looks around, baffled, wondering how he got outside of a random San-van house.

He hears a child crying from inside. "Father!"

He runs inside, passes the bathroom on the left, and hears it again. "Father, no!" The child weeps.

Turning to the right towards the living room, he sees pictures of Lily and Luke on the walls.

Roscoe scans the room. "What the hell is this?" He yells, "Lily, are you here?"

He makes his way into the kitchen. He sees blood everywhere and a little girl with her back to him holding a man's head as she is crying.

"Father, get up." She weeps.

Roscoe puts his hand on her shoulder. She looks up at him and recognizes him. "Roscoe, what are you doing here? How is this possible?"

Roscoe replies, "Lil? I don't know," as he disappears

from her dream.

He awakes back on the Dark Wolf and watches Lily

as she wakes up.

Confused by what happened, she yells at Roscoe.

"What the hell was that?"

Roscoe gets up from the blanket on the floor, puts

on his pants, starts to pace, and utters, "You just

dreamed…"

She sits up with the top blanket covering her,

shocked by what he said. "How could that be?"

He looks at her and replies, "I'm guessing because

you have not taken your pills."

She rubs her head and says, "OK, but that does not

explain how you were there?"

Looking down in shame, Roscoe answers, "Because

I think I can Dream Weave."

Perplexed by it all, Lily gets up quickly and gets dressed. "So, how long have you been able to do this?"

Roscoe, frightened of how she will respond, replies, "I guess the first time you woke me up."

Lily thinks for a second. She backs up towards the door, furious with him. "Wait. You mean when I woke you up just as we were entering, Ma'de?"

Moving toward her with his hand out, Roscoe pleads with her, "Yes, I'm so sorry. I didn't know they would be able to know where I was."

Lily pushes his hand away and says, "My father is dead, and my mother, who the hell knows where? Why didn't you just say something?" Lily begins to tear up.

Roscoe pleaded with her, "I didn't know who to trust! I didn't know what was happening to me! Please understand, I never wanted any of this to happen." His arms stretched out.

Randi comes over the intercom and says, "We have arrived at Newwart."

Standing by the medical bay door, Lily asks, "Why didn't you tell me after we got to know each other?"

"I tried many times but couldn't find the words for what was happening to me."

"I can't do this right now," she says as he walks over to touch her. "No, don't touch me. I don't want to talk to you right now." Tears rolling down her face.

Roscoe follows her closely as she leaves. "Lily, wait, Lily, wait!" Ignoring him, she keeps walking down the hall.

Jeff comes out of his room, drinking a bottle of rum already in his snow gear. "Glad she is okay."

Roscoe sighs, disheartened, as they walk down the hall of the Dark Wolf. "Yeah, I'm glad she is too."

Jeff slaps him on the back. "What? Have lady problems, or does it have to do with you going all blue earlier? That was some crazy stuff." He takes another drink before offering it to Roscoe.

Roscoe shakes his head, takes a sip, and coughs. "Both."

Randi comes over the intercom. "We have arrived at the Highyeah base, Captain Mitchell."

"I guess we will have to wait till next time to talk, and you need to change into your snow gear."

Feeling saddened by the pain he caused Lily and more alone than ever, Roscoe says, "You are right. I'm going to change and meet you in the loading hangar." He hands the bottle back to Jeff.

Jeff takes another drink. "Roger that, remember I'm here for you, Roscoe."

Roscoe gets to his room, gets ready, and heads to the loading area.

You could feel the tension coming off him and Lily as he entered the room.

Ophelia, sitting next to Lily, leans over. "Hey, is everything okay?"

Lily looks over at Roscoe and says, "Ask him." The loading door opens, and she puts her blaster in her holster and steps off.

Roscoe steps towards her and says, "Lil."

Commander Athena comes running up.

She says, "Captain, Dr. Beal said she needs you to

come to Hara when you arrive immediately."

Looking at the sky, Captain Mitchell says, "It looks

clear enough to take the drop ship down into Hara. When

did they leave?"

She responds, "A few days back, they took the Snow

speeders and went through the Dark hair forest.

Captain Mitchell says, "If we go now, we should get

there as soon as they arrive." They get back on the Dark

Wolf and head down to Hara.

Dr. Beal wakes up, hears blaster fire, and comes out

of her tent to see the soldier watching Henry practice

shooting. She walks up to Henry and watches. He misses

the target.

"Take a deep breath, and on the exhale, squeeze the trigger. Henry does it and hits the target.

"Wow, you are good," he says excitedly to her.

"My father wanted sons," she says, walking away. "Let's go; we need to head out. We should be in Hara in about twelve hours, and everyone else should be there by now."

Henry, rubbing the snow from his knee, gets up and replies, "OK, right away, let me pack up my sack and get my gear ready."

She puts more stuff in her pack. "We'll move out in five minutes."

Henry walks up to Dr. Beal, and the imperial soldier says, "So when Roscoe gets here, will you tell him or wait until we return to space?" They tie the slide to one of the speeders.

While putting her pack on her back, Dr. Beal responds, "We will figure out this food warehouse situation, and then I will tell him."

Henry climbs on the back of her Snow speeder and says, "I'm with you. We don't know why she is hunting him now. I will do whatever you think is best." This shows how much he has grown to trust her after all that has happened. They speed off into the snow toward Hara.

The Dark Wolf flies overhead as they reach the clearing of the Darkhair forest. They see the Town of Hara in the distance.

Dr. Beal and Henry look up and see the Dark Wolf overhead, "There they go," she says.

As the Dark Wolf lands on the Hara outpost, The Four Trees, which have four giant Bayhi trees on the four corners of the post with a wall, make up the base's outer shield. The next layer is the outer stone wall in the Bayhi trees; the last layer is the base itself, which has a command room with cameras of everything in and out of Hara. They also have a gate to the north to keep Reavers from heading south to Hara with snipers in all four trees.

Commander Turner of the Four Trees post walks up

with two other soldiers and tells Captain

Mitchell as he exits the Dark Wolf, "Sir Chancellor

Gann has left Hara. I'm in charge in his absence. What can

I do for you and your team, Captain?"

Still trying to get Lily to speak to him, Roscoe tries

to get her attention. "Psst, hey Lily, can I talk to you for

five minutes, please?" as they step off the Dark Wolf.

Lily, still infuriated with him, gives him a hateful

look and says, "Not the time, Roscoe."

Razor looks back and says, "Lock it up. Something is

wrong here."

Luke bites into an apple and says, "Yeah, something

is up. Strangely, the Chancellor said he would be here. Then

he just up and leaves without saying anything. Why?"

Captain Mitchell questioned the Commander, "He is

right that it is strange for him to leave knowing we were

coming. Where is Chancellor Gann? He was supposed to

brief us on the attacks on the food warehouse."

The commander acts shady and says, "He is my

boss, he doesn't tell me where he is going."

Ophelia intervenes and says, "Sure, we will go with that. Do you know when he will return?"

Commander Turner, rubbing his chin, glances back at her and says, "Nope, he did not tell me when he would be back either. " He then turns his head to look at her.

Irritated by the commander's attitude, Captain Mitchell grabs him by the shirt, lifts him off his feet, and says, "In the name of the emperor, tell us?"

He shivers and says, "Like I said, Captain, I have no clue."

"Fine, did Dr. Beal and a kid show up yet?"

"I can look if you would put me down. But first, I must get out of this blasted damn cold."

Captain Mitchell puts him down, and Commander Turner jerks away, fixes his jacket, and says, "Follow me." Then, he walks away from Captain Mitchell.

The team follows him to the entrance of the Four Trees. They pass the command center and then enter the

Commander's office. He sits down and brings up some cameras from inside his desk.

He looks at the cameras. "Captain, she has not arrived yet. I can have one of my men take you to the front gate to see if you can see them coming down the mountain."

Captain Mitchell turns around as he leaves and says, "Thanks for all your help, Commander. I hope not to see you again," he says harshly.

As they descend the hall of the Four Trees, a horn sounds at the main gate. It goes off four times, signaling that someone is injured, and everyone runs to the north gate to investigate. When the team arrives, Dr. Beal, Henry, and an injured imperial soldier are walking in.

Roscoe runs up to Henry, embraces him, and says, "My friend, you look just as bad as you smell. Whew!" Roscoe plugs his nose and steps back.

Henry pulls Roscoe close, hugs him tightly, and says, "You have no idea. You look strong now, kinda buff?"

"Yeah, I have been training with Sergeant Razor." Roscoe shows off his muscles.

"You look much better, man. I'm glad to see that you made it."

Walking next to Henry, Roscoe says, "You too. The things that have happened to me these past few months we could not have imagined as kids at St. Ethel's." He looks over at Lily.

Henry's expression is saddened, and says, "Yeah, but some things are a lot different in real life than when we were playing as kids." Henry notices how Roscoe looks at Lily and says, "So, what's up with that?"

Looking back at Henry, worried about him, Roscoe says, "Are you all good, brother?

Henry's face suddenly becomes stern. He rubs a tear from his eyes and says, "Yes, it's just cold out here. So, what's going on with you and blondie?"

"It's complicated," the two old friends walk to the gate.

"I hope you can figure it out. You can lose someone at the drop of a hat." He stares off into the distance.

Roscoe looks him up and down and says, "OK. " He thinks about how different he and his friend have become and feels it was all his fault.

Henry changed the subject. "Man, I'm ready for some soup. It's so cold."

Dr. Beal removes and cleans her glasses as she and Cap walk ahead of Roscoe and Henry.

As he walks alongside her, she asks Captain Mitchell, "How is he? He seems different."

As they approach the door, Captain Mitchell says,

"He is becoming a great soldier, but something else is starting to happen to him; I think we need to tell him the truth."

As the Commander approaches them, Dr. Beal says, "Hold on. We will deal with that after we deal with what the emperor sent us here for.

Where is Chancellor Gann?" She looks confused as

he approaches them.

The Commander says, "Like I said to your friends earlier, he has left, and I do not know when he will be back either," being very short with her.

She looks very complex. "That is so weird. Chancellor Gann knew I was coming on behalf of the emperor to deal with the food bank attacks."

"That is what I told him," Captain Mitchell says to her.

As they walk down the hall to the medical bay, he says, "I have had no report on any food Warehouse attacks?"

They walk up to the medical bay and drop off the injured soldier, and Luke says, "I feel someone is playing a game, and we are pawns in it."

Jeff lights his cigar and says, "I'm with him. I feel like we are playing someone else's game, boss. We need to find out who is behind this."

Razor looks at Jeff and says, "Put that out, fool. We

have bigger things to deal with."

Captain Mitchell looks at the commander and asks, "Where is the chow hall? We need some food."

Itching for a fight now, Lily says, "Cap, he is lying."

Luke nudges her and says, "Lily, let it go, it's not the time."

Lily presses the Commander. "Come on, tell us the truth."

Luke says, "What is wrong with you?" but she ignores him.

The Commander laughs and says, "Yeah, listen to him, girl, stay in your place."

Luke puts his hand on his gun and says, "Commander, with all due respect, do not talk to my sister like that again, or you will lose your tongue."

Ophelia steps in between them and Commander Turner and says, "Back up."

Captain Mitchell puts his hand on Lily's shoulders,

calming her down. "Where is the chow hall, Commander, please?"

The Commander snickers and says, "Around the corner and to the left, enjoy."

As she passes him, Dr. Beal shakes her head and says, "Let's go, ladies. I'm hungry and have missed you two."

Ophelia bumps the Commander as she walks by and says, "Next time, little man."

Commander Turner blows a kiss at her and replies, "Hopefully soon, as he stares at Luke and everyone as they pass by.

They arrive at the chow hall, grab food, and sit at a long table with chairs on either side.

Jeff says as he sits down, "Yes, soup. I can use something warm."

Roscoe sits down with Lily across from him, reaches his hand out to her hand, and says, "Lil, can we please go somewhere and talk now?"

Lily pulls her hand off the table and yells at him, "I told you not right now, but since you can't listen, let's just talk right here in front of everyone."

Roscoe pleads with her. "No, Lil, please do not do this, not like this."

She stands up and says, "No, why not? You want to talk so bad, let's. Everyone, Roscoe has been Dream weaving." She breaks down a little. " Just because he is so afraid to trust anyone. My family is gone!"

Luke walks up to Roscoe and punches him, knocking him to the ground. Razor and Ophelia grab him. Pulling him back, he yells, "You coward, everything is all your fault."

Henry bends over to check on Roscoe, helps him to his feet, and says, "You need to tell him now." He looks over at Dr. Beal

Dr. Beal looks over at Captain Mitchell, and he nods his head.

Roscoe wipes the blood off his face, looking at Cap

and Dr. Beal confused. "Henry, what are you talking about? What is going on?"

Dr. Beal puts her head down. "The woman you keep seeing." She pauses.

Roscoe becomes very curious, and he says, "Yes?"

Dr. Beal sighs and replies, "She is your mother." Everyone stands there shocked, except Captain Mitchell.

Seeing that he already knew, Roscoe yells, "You knew, didn't you?"

Captain Mitchell walks towards him and replies, "Son, we were just trying to do what we thought was best."

Roscoe backed up, became defensive, and said, "I'm not your son. " Then, he begins to feel his blue energy radiating around him.

Henry reaches out his hand and says, "Roscoe, you need to calm down; she had her reasons."

Looking at him sideways, Roscoe becomes angrier and charges up. "You are taking her side now, my so-called brother!"

Henry pleads with him as he steps away, saying, "You don't understand. You need to hear her out. I trust her with my life; she is a good person and had a good reason."

Feeling alone and furious, Roscoe replies, "I mean nothing to you people, do I?"

With his arms out, Razor says, "Come on, kid, you know that is not true."

Roscoe looks at him and calms down momentarily as Dr. Beal walks closer. "Roscoe, we are your family."

Roscoe looks over at Lily, but she does not look at him. He says, "I'm so sorry, but no," and disappears into a cloud of blue smoke that consumes him.

Dr. Beal falls to her knees and says, "Oh no, what have I done?" They all stand there in disbelief.

Chapter 7

Roscoe appears again at the edge of the Darkhair forest. He looks back at the post and pauses for a minute, thinking about returning. Furious with others, he turns around, steps into the forest, and kneels. He closes his eyes. "Mother."

Rachel, on her ship just behind Yule, the ice moon, the second of Newwart's moons, hears Roscoe calling out to her.

She looks at her pilot. "Get me to the Darkhair forest now! Something has changed, and this might be my time to take him." She kneels and closes her eyes. "I am here, my son." They both appear in a solid white room.

Looking at her, Roscoe says, "Can you take your hood off, please?

Rachel takes her hood off as Roscoe walks over, seeing her pale, freckled face with a dimple on her right cheek for the first time. Roscoe places his hand on her shoulder, staring into her blue-gray eyes. "Mom."

She touches his hand. "I'm here, my son." Trying to manipulate him and get him to lower his guard as her drop ship draws near Newwart.

Roscoe drops his hand, looks down, and walks away from her in dismay. "Where have you been, and why did you leave me? Did you not love me?"

"Because I love you, Roscoe, I had to leave you."

"What kind of answer is that?" Roscoe becomes angry. He begins to pace the room, increasingly angry, "Look, you owe me more than that!"

"Roscoe, listen, they left me no choice. When your great uncle became The Dream King, I did not believe in his plan until the Emperor tried to punish me for something I didn't do, so I went to my uncle, who gifted me with the power I needed to get my revenge. I had to get back at the people who took everything from me."

Roscoe grows impatient. "So, what does all that have to do with me?"

"Everything." She turns and walks away from Roscoe. "He gifted me with his power. One drop of his blood and I was like him. But what I didn't know was I was carrying you, and it passed through my blood to you. Your blood is the blood of The Dream King, and he wants you. I couldn't let that happen."

Roscoe gets frustrated. "What the hell does he want from me!"

She looks around as the void cracks a little. "Calm down, and I will explain." Roscoe calms his breathing, and then the void becomes stable again. "He wants you to be his vessel back into this realm."

"Why am I so special? Why not you?"

"You are the last living male heir from his bloodline. Since I found out I have been trying to protect you."

Roscoe throws his hands up. "Protect me! You call trying to kill me, protecting me?" The void rattles. Roscoe screams falling to his knees. "I can't control what's inside of me." Overwhelmed by his power, a blue flame surrounds him.

She places her hand on his head. "You are losing control. Focus Roscoe! Listen to my voice!"

Roscoe grabbed her arm tight, and his eyes began to glow blue. He said, "What the hell does that mean? Just tell me how to control it."

She pulls his hands off her, grabs his hand, lifts him from his knees, and says, "Let go of your fear of letting people down. I am sorry I left you. I wish it could have been different, but it wasn't. You must be ready. He will send others and will do whatever it takes to get you."

As he listens, the rattling stops, and the flame around him diminishes. "So, what are you here for, to do his bidding?"

"No, Roscoe, but I will do what I must."
Roscoe's fingers begin to spark. "I'm not afraid of anything or anyone; I am ready."

She walks past him, "You keep telling yourself that, kid. You should be afraid. He will kill everyone you love, even that girl of yours. He sees everything in our dreams."

Roscoe gets mad again and yells, "He better not

touch her. I'll kill him," the void cracks again.

She looks around, her hands spread out. "See, you

can't control it. He will use that against you." She multiplies

and surrounds him. "You can't save them. He will kill her

with your hands. You are too weak."

Roscoe shakes his head. "No! I'm not weak. Just

help me! Stop with all the mind games!" A burst of energy

comes out of him, shooting in all directions.

She slaps the energy bursts across the room. "Good,

Roscoe. With some training, you might have a chance.

Calm your breathing and clear your mind."

Roscoe takes a deep breath and closes his eyes.

When he does, Rachel starts to see a glimpse of Lily and

the others in the void.

She shakes her head. "You disappoint me. Do you

think she will forgive you? Do you think any of them will?

You have and will cause them so much pain. Just come

with me."

Roscoe breaks his focus. "Shut up. You don't know her or them. I would never just abandon them like you did me." and the void begins to break down again.

She looks at him and says, "You are too weak and now I must do what I have too." Her ship enters Newwart's atmosphere.

He walks towards her to grab her, but she disappears. He says, "What does that mean?"

At the post, alarms go off, and Jeff says, "What now?"

A soldier comes over the intercom. "Commander Turner, we have an unmarked drop ship headed for the Highyeah Mountains. It should be here in no time."

Dr. Beal freaks out. "Oh no, Roscoe!" She runs out of the chow hall, heads to the motor yard, and runs towards a speeder.

Lily looks at everyone and says, "I'll go with her. You guys get the Dark Wolf and shoot that son of a bitch out of the sky." As she runs out to catch up with her, she says, "I'll drive. I may be mad at him right now, but I love him."

Dr. Beal moves to the back of the speeder and says, "I know. I just hope we make it in time." They zoom off towards the Darkhair forest.

As the void continues to collapse, Roscoe yells at his mother. "Rachel, where are you? Tell me now!"
Back on her ship, she yells, "Get me down there now!" Her ship zooms by the Highyeah mountains.

Roscoe kneels, breathing hard in the snow as steam rolls off him. He looks up and sees the light of a drop-ship over him. Rachel descends into the Darkhair forest on a rope ladder.

Dr. Beal and Lily, just a little way out from the Darkhair forest, see this, too. Dr. Beal says, "Hurry, she will get him." Lily speeds up, and they blast off even faster.

Roscoe, still kneeling in the snow, and Rachel reaches the ground.

She approaches him. "You're coming with me."

Roscoe stands up, wipes himself off, gets in a fighting stance, and says, "I don't understand why you are doing this, but you can come and try it."

Dr. Beal and Lily show up at the Darkhair forest, and the snow continues to fall.

Dr. Beal looks at him, showing concern, and says, "Roscoe, are you okay?"

Rachel looks at them as she walks closer to Roscoe and says, "You think you can save him like you tried to with me, Brooklyn? Well, no one can save my son. He wants him."

Dr. Beal pleads with her, "I loved you and tried to save you, and you know it. You chose him."

Rachel, getting angry, says, "You chose to follow the people who killed the love of my life and ruined my family, the family that could have had!" She turns towards Dr. Beal and Lily.

Dr. Beal tells her, "I was doing what I thought was right. We had no proof of what you claimed. She is the princess."

"You were my friend," Rachel screams. "That should have been enough."

Lily pulls her pistol blaster and says, "Enough with all this back and forth. She ruined my family. She needs to die." Lily fires at Rachel.

She dodges all of them and shadow jumps all over the place.

Rachel stops, pulls out her blaster, says, "Stupid girl," and fires at Lily and Dr. Beal.

Roscoe yells, "No!" and he shadow jumps in front of them, taking a blast in his abdomen.

Roscoe, standing there with a hole in his abdomen, spits up blood and says, "Lily, I love you." as he falls to the ground, the snow becomes dark red around him.

Rachel turns around and walks away as a tear rolls down her face.

Lily and Dr. Beal drop to their knees over the top of him, putting pressure on his wound.

Lily looks up at Rachel and yells, "Save him, please save him. I know you can," and she cries.

Rachel stops and pauses for a second, and she pulls her hood back up and starts to walk away, replying, "He is dead. Let him go."

Dr. Beal holds her hands on Roscoe's wound as blood pours out and says, "He is your son. Does that mean nothing to you?"

Rachel says, "He means more to me than you will ever know." She whispers, "May we meet in the stars, son." Then, she disappears into the forest and returns to her ship.

The Dark Wolf drops from the clouds above just behind the unmarked drop ship, and Captain Mitchell yells, "Open fire!" as cannon and blaster fire rain upon it.

They take a hit as Rachel returns to the cabin and yells, "Get us the hell out of here now!"

The pilot of her ship says, "I'm trying, General." Attempting to evade the Dark Wolf.

As she sits down in her chair, they take another hit,

and she says, "Try harder, or I'll find a new pilot."

Frantically trying to save Roscoe's life, Dr. Beal

radios the Dark Wolf, "Dark Wolf, this is Dr. Beal. Over."

Captain Mitchell, on the tail of the other drop ship,

says, "This is the Dark Wolf. We read you.

"We need you guys right now! Roscoe is hurt.

Over."

"We have her. We can capture her and figure out

their plans."

In a panic voice, Dr. Beal yells, "Roscoe is dying. We need

you to meet us in the clearing to the west of us now!" Just

then, Roscoe passes out.

Captain Mitchell worries about him and orders Luke

to get the Dark Wolf there. "Take us to their location

now!"

Luke turns the Dark Wolf west and says, "Yes, sir, but she

is getting away."

Captain Mitchell watches the other ship fly out of

Newwart's atmosphere and says, "I promise you we will

end this soon and bring her in for what she has done."

Dr. Beal looks at Lily and says, "We must move him to that clearing. They will meet us there. Let's go."

They transfer him to the speeder and hurry. When they arrive, the Dark Wolf is waiting. They return to the ship and place him in the medical tube.

Dr. Beal pushes the buttons to start diagnostics on him and says, "Randi, what are his vitals?"

"I'm sorry, doctor. Nothing," Randi replies. A flat line appears on the screen.

Lily breaks down crying, "Don't tell me that," while Ophelia comforts her.

Dr. Beal says, "Randi, shock him now." She does, and nothing happens. "Again!"

Roscoe's body starts to levitate and glow as a bright blue shield surrounds it, and then he falls back down— beep, *beep*. The monitor picks up a heartbeat.

Jeff freaking out, says, "Randi, what the hell was that?"

Randi says, "That was not me. As far as I can see, he is stable now, but he lost a lot of blood. I don't know if or when he will wake."

Dr. Beal sighs, looking down at her blood-stained hands and clothes, "I don't care. He is safe. That's what matters. He will pull through this." She looks at him and places her hand on the glass as his vitals pass. "Randi takes some of his blood. I will need to examine it in my lab later. I'm going to shower."

Lily pulls a chair up and says, "I'll stay with him for now."

Ophelia leaves the room and says, "I'll get you some food. We grabbed some supplies from the post."

Luke looks at Razor and says, "Do you want to go spar? I need to let out some frustration," as they leave the medical bay.

Jeff says, "Hang in there, kid, and looks over at Henry and says, "Come on, he will be ok. I'll show you to your room."

Captain Mitchell puts his hand on the tube and says, "Randi, set a course for Rydean."

Randi says, "Right away, sir, the ship shoots off towards Rydean.

Meanwhile, Chancellor Gann is on his drop-ship, which is more luxurious but slower than the Dark Wolf but still packed with all the weaponry.

He is drawing near to Jade, Lanard's moon, when the pilot says, "Chancellor, you are being hailed."

He gets up and heads to leave the bridge and says, "I'll take it in my quarters." He gets to his room and presses a button on the wall. A hologram comes up, and a person in a hood stands there.

Chancellor Gann paces in his room, arms folded in the sleeves of his orange and black Reaver fur-covered robe, and says, "I'm almost to Lanard. Is everything ready to go?"

The cloaked figure says, "Yes, we are. She told me

the shipment should be good, do it."

Chancellor Gann hangs up, walks to the speaker by his door, and says, "Pilot, take us down to the post-Asura outside of Kast."

The pilot says, "Yes, sir," as the chancellor's ship descends into Lanard and then into the post-Asura. The location was just a little post with a drop-ship dockyard and a small building with two towers, one on either side. No more than thirty soldiers were assigned here.

As the Chancellor's ship lands, all the soldiers come out, line up on either side, and salute him as he passes.

Commander Smith of the post approaches him. "Hello, Chancellor. It's late. I didn't get a notification about a drop-ship arriving this late, or I would have had us out here before you landed."

Chancellor Gann waves his hand and says, "It's my fault. I wanted to see Chancellor Docain before the summit, and if I'm being honest, this is my favorite time of the year here. The Cockapee migration is divine. So, it was one of those spur-of-the-moment things."

Commander Smith, walking alongside him into the post as he holds the door open for him, says, "Oh, sorry, sir, she is not in Kast."

Chancellor Gann turns around and says, "Where is she then?"

Walking up to him, Commander Smith says, "She is at her estate in Cooperton. Would you like a ride, sir? We can get you a Wing guider up in 5 minutes."

Chancellor Gann sits on a bench in the hall, puts his leg over the other, and says, "Yes, that would be wonderful. It's a nice night. I like the cool air of the desert."

The Wing guider lands, Chancellor Gann gets in, and it takes off. They land outside her estate, a white marble stone palace with four towers on each corner. Grand windows in front of the palace have stained glass murals of the Creator and all the planets surrounding him as if he were the sun. The palace also has a courtyard in the middle with plants and flowers hanging from the balconies. A canopy covers a side patio so Chancellor Docain can watch the Cockapee migrate from her chair.

As Chancellor's Docain guards walked through the Lanardin sand to the Wing guider, they saluted him. "Chancellor Gann, we didn't know you were coming. Let me radio and let them know you are here."

The guard puts his hand on his ear and says, "Mr. Fred, we have a visitor. It's Chancellor Gann."

Mr. Fred, a lean man with tan skin wearing a red suit and red suede shoes matching his short red hair, is the right-hand man of the Docain family. He walked briskly across the marble stone courtyard and up the stairs to Chancellor Docain's door, knocked, and said, "Ma'am, Chancellor Gann is here to see you."

She stands in her milk bath, covered in red and yellow striped Kast desert flower petals, and says, "Fred, I just got in. Do you have any idea what he wants?"

Standing outside the door with his ear pressed against it, Fred says, "I do not know, Ma'am. Do you want me to find out?"

She grabbed her towel at the foot of her tub, wrapped it around herself, and said, "It's fine. I'll just receive him on the patio."

Mr. Fred walks away and says, "Yes, ma'am, I'll walk him out there now."

Chancellor Docain walks out of the double doors leading to the patio. She is tall, long-legged, yellow-skinned, hazel-eyed, with long, straight red hair and a black dot on her left cheek. People say she is the most beautiful woman in Lanard. She walks down the patio wearing a white, burgundy dress with gold high heels, which knocks on the stone path as Chancellor Gann watches.

Once she arrives, he stands up and says, "Chancellor Docain, you are as stunning as ever." He then kisses her hand.

She sits down and says, "Don't flatter me. What can I do for you at this late hour?"

Chancellor Gann reaches into the bag he brought

with him and grabs a bottle. "I just got the new batch of wine for this season, and I know how you like your wines. I figured I would stop by before seeing the Cockapee migration."

She waves over Mr. Fred. "Bring us some glasses, please."

Chancellor Gann reaches into his bag again, pulls out two glasses, and says, "No need. I got it. I came prepared," and poured the wine.

She looks back at Mr. Fred and says, "You are good, thank you."

Before leaving, he says, "I'll be right inside if you need anything," bowing his head before walking away.

She looks at Chancellor Gann and says, "So what are you here for?" She smells the wine in her glass.

He sits, smells the wine, takes a sip, and then says, "So, have you given any thought to our proposal?"

She crosses her legs and drinks while looking through her long gold binoculars, watching the Cockapees cross the desert sands of Lanard. A full moon hangs in the background. She says, "So beautiful. You know what I love about the Cockapee, Chancellor?"

"No, what," he says.

She takes another sip and says, "They know their place in the herd, and what you speak of is treason and is punishable by death." She coughs up blood all over the table, and she yells to him, "What did you do to me?" She looks at her glass and falls over.

He walks over to her glass and pours out the wine. He puts the cup back in his bag and says, "I thought you would say that. I didn't want this. You made me do this, and she did, too. All we want is not to be ruled by another murderous tyrant."

"You don't know if it was her or not, Gann." She coughs up more blood. "What are you guys planning to do, march to the palace and take it? She will for sure kill you all," as she continues to cough.

He kneels by her, stating, "Have you ever lost a child

before? No? You wouldn't know. My life means nothing to me. Getting my revenge and taking from her what she loves is all that matters to me, and we will do that exact thing.

"What's that," she says as she begins to suffocate on her blood.

He leans in and whispers to her, "Her Power!"

"Order 23," she gasped as her life fled her body.

"May we meet in the stars," he says as he closes her eyes. Then he stands back up and yells, "Help someone, help!" Two guards come running up.

One of the guards says, "Chancellor Gann, are you ok?"

He coughs and says, "Yes, my boy, but I couldn't save her," as Mr. Fred walks up.

He points at Mr. Fred and says, "That Jaair, did it. Arrest him now!"

Mr. Fred, pleading with the guards, says, "You know me, I would never, but it fell on deaf ears because the Chancellor had already paid them off.

Chancellor Gann says, "Take him away to Hara. I'll deal with him there. Prepare my ship."

" Yes, Chancellor," the guards reply.

He boards a Wing Guider and flies off.

Chapter 8

"I should have told him sooner," Captain Mitchell thinks to himself as he stares out the bridge of the Dark Wolf. He felt the full weight of his decision.

Dr. Beal enters the cabin. Seeing the anguish on his face, she puts her hand on his shoulder and says, "My friend, it is not on you. It was my call. You have to let this one go."

Stepping closer to the window, he leans one arm against it, looking at the stars. "I know, but he was under my care, and he got hurt."

"People get hurt, Cap. You know this: it comes with the job. What about this kid has got you all twisted up?" she says.

Captain Mitchell sighs. "He is special and is showing incredible progress."

She replies, "I'm starting to see that. What was that blue energy around him? It looks like Rachel's."

"It started on Ma'de and only grew. Last month, he saved Lily from a frozen lake and had that all around him when they came up."

"I need to check on his blood work. Maybe we will find some answers there."

"Yeah, I just hope he pulls through."

"He will. Did you feel like something was up at the post? Why would Chancellor Gann not be there?" Dr. Beal walks toward the center map.

Captain Mitchell turns around and walks back towards her. "Yeah, I saw some of the other Chancellors, and they were acting off as well."

Dr. Beal says, "We will need to look into this after we get done fixing the Sun. They should all be at the summit next weekend, and we can get to the bottom of it there."

Captain Mitchell sits in his seat. "Regarding that, I got us a smuggler to handle our builder problem, so when we get to Rydean, we should be able to build the portal and finally end this."

Dr. Beal picks up and looks at the power core on the center island. "That's well and good, but how do we stop him and her without Roscoe?"

He stands, grabs her hand, and says, "He will wake up, and we will defeat him and heal the sun. Everything will be ok."

She replies, "You are right. We can do anything together. Thanks. I will head to my lab to check his blood."

"Anytime I'm going to get some food, see ya," Captain Mitchell replies.

"Bye," She replies, leaving the bridge. Captain Mitchell walks past the medical bay and sees Ophelia sitting beside Roscoe's bed. He steps in to check on Roscoe. "How is he doing?"

She stands up to attention and says, "Same, sir, I just thought I would come talk to him. Keep him company while Lily rests."

"Good idea, soldier, carry on." He leaves and heads

to the chow hall.

Ophelia stands over Roscoe's tub, "I know we haven't spent much time together getting to know each other, and that might be my fault. I'm a little closed off and don't trust people easily, but we share that, I see. I'll try to improve on my end. You love Lily. I can see that. She loves you, so I'll give you guys a real chance when you wake. So come on already, kid, and wake up," placing her hand on his tub.

As the rest of the team is in the chow hall, Captain Mitchell enters and says, "Hey guys, Ophelia is in the medical bay, and someone needs to relieve her just in case he wakes up."

Luke gets up and puts his bowl in the sink. "I got it, Cap."

Luke hesitantly walks down the hall to the medical bay, not knowing what he wants to say. He fights the fact that Roscoe's mother contributed to his family's falling apart, but he also saved Lily.

He arrives at the medical bay and the door opens. "I got you, O, go get you some food."

She gets up to leave and places her hand on the tub. "Thanks, Luke. See you soon, kid. Get better," and she leaves the room.

Luke walks up to his tub and places his hand on it. "I know I have given you a hard time, and I punched you in the face. I'm truly sorry for that. I know now it's not your fault what happened to my parents. You were kept in the dark about the truth, and I would not trust us either." He gets up and walks around. "Oh, thank you so much for saving Lily. I don't know what I would do without her. I owe you, brother," he walks back over and sits down.

The next morning, as the Dark Wolf passes by Izeal, Henry stares out the window of the medical bay, seeing the lights of his home. He reminisces on how much he loved Sister Ethel's oatmeal raisin cookies.

Henry sighs and turns around, walking back towards Roscoe. He sits beside him and says, "There it is, Roscoe, home. It looks a lot brighter from up here. It's crazy how much we have changed since we last saw it. I wish you could see it. I was just thinking about sister Ethel's cookies." He laughs to himself and then says, "Remember that time she told us not to eat them, and you wouldn't listen, and you took one early and it burned the hell out of your mouth, I can see it now" and he laughs again. His mood becomes somber, saying, "That's when life was simpler." He pauses, stands up, and starts to pace the room, "I made a mistake that cost people's lives. I think about that night every day now. I don't know if I could return to work at a plant again. My life must be more than that. I must atone for the lives that are on me. I must be better. I can't freeze again. I wish you were up to talk to me and train with me. Roscoe, I miss you, buddy. Please wake up." He walks back to the window and looks at Izeal as it passes.

Chancellor Gann's drop ship enters the Four Trees, and Commander Turner walks out to greet him. Chancellor Gann and two guards are walking Mr. Fred in handcuffs.

The Commander approaches them, "Sir, welcome back. What would you like me to do with him?"

He hands Mr. Fred over, "He will be our guest for a while. Try to make him as comfortable as possible. " He laughs.

"Yes, sir," Commander Turner laughs.

"What did the honorable Captain Mitchell say?"

"He was none too pleased, sir. He and Dr. Beal were asking why you left when you knew they were coming," he said as he walked Mr. Fred into the post.

The Chancellor, heading to the takeoff pad to a Wing guider, said, "The Emperor trusts them and keeps us on the outs, but soon things will be different. I'm going to go to Hara to get packed for the summit. You deal with him," pointing at Mr. Fred.

The commander leads Mr. Fred downstairs to the

dungeon, which is dark, damp, and cold. The little light they get comes from the bars on the windows in each cell. He throws him in one and says, "I hope you enjoy your new home," before slamming the door behind him.

Mr. Fred stands up, runs to the cell entrance, and screams, "No, you can't do this to me. I am a citizen of the empire; I deserve a trial. You hear me!"

The Dark Wolf enters Rydean's atmosphere. Sitting in his chair, Captain Mitchell tells Randi, "Hale Morereck, it is one of the oldest posts in the galaxy, second in size only to the magnificent Galideal off of Izeal.

Randi replies, "Yes, sir," as she hails Morereck.

Morereck's chief of communication radios in. "Name and call sign, please?"

Captain Mitchell leans up before replying, "Captain Mitchell of the Dark Wolf requesting permission to land?"

She replies, "Permission granted, welcome back to Morereck, Captain Mitchell."

The Dark Wolf begins its descent upon Morereck, Captain Mitchell and the team gather in the loading deck preparing their gear, including Dr. Beal, who was in her lab.

"What is that?" Dr. Beal examines Roscoe's blood closer and sees purple crystals on his red and white blood cells. She jumps from her desk and looks at Roscoe through the glass that separates the medical bay from her lab.

"What are you?" she asks, examining his blood again. Randi runs his blood through the system again."

"Yes Doctor, what am I looking for?"

"I don't know, just look for anything abnormal." Dr. Beal sits down and turns in her chair, looking at Roscoe's blood.

"Excuse me, Dr. Beal, I have found a DNA match for him in the database."

"You should, Randi. Rachel got her blood drawn at the Academy like we all did."

"No, Ma'am, there are multiple DNA matches for him."

Dr. Beal, surprised by this revelation, says, "Show me, Randi,"

"Oh, my Creator, it all makes sense to me now. Delete this now! Take his sample out of the database. No one can know about his lineage."

"Yes, Dr. Beal," Randi replies. Dr. Beal takes notes in her journal and exits the lab as she deletes him from the database.

` Captain Mitchell orders as Dr. Beal finally arrives, "Good, you are here. We will do this: Luke, Razor, Ophelia, Jeff, Henry, and I will meet up with Tekey-Espy and the builder in Bearsekk. Lily, you and Dr. Beal will stay here, get the supplies we need, and have everything ready to build the portal. We need to get there as fast as possible."

Shocked by Cap's decision to leave her behind, Lily says, "Cap, what's up? What did I do? Why do I have to stay back?"

Cap looks at everyone and says, "You have your orders. Get ready to go. We should be landing soon."

"Yes, sir." Everyone else goes back to packing

their gear.

Cap looks at Lily and says, "Come here." They walk over to the door together. "I thought you would want to be here when he wakes up."

She snaps quickly and says, "Yes, but I'm still a soldier."

"You are going to want to be here when he wakes."

"If he wakes up, you mean," she says before turning and walking away.

Dr. Beal hears what Lily said to him and walks up to Cap, "She is hurting. I got her. Go get them."

"Ok, just let her know how she is," he replies.

The Dark Wolf lowers onto the platform on the post of Morereck, which is surrounded by two walls in the shape of a square. The outer square is the newer and the bigger of the two. The wall is made from stones from the caves of Rydean and Windomm. It has a tower on each of the four corners, which is patrolled by two guards and a man blaster turret with complete 360-degree rotation on top of the towers. So, they can see the center of the post as well as the outside of it. A hundred yards separate the outer wall from the inner wall. This part houses the drop-ship yard, the general sleeping quarters, and the infirmary. The inner wall was built by the Rydeanins ages ago to withstand the elements. It was made from stone from the caves throughout Rydean as well, which is where the cities are. Emperor Colten Cascade and his brother Victor destroyed parts of it when a Rydean tribe stole their sister Jenny and held her there. She was never seen again. The Command center, armory, chow hall, and Commander's quarters are in the inner wall.

Sitting next to Henry, Jeff begins to spray himself heavily with bug spray, which causes Henry to start coughing uncontrollably.

Henry looks at Jeff and says, "Yo, you think you got enough, dang," as he coughs again.

Jeff throws him the spray and says, "You better put it on. I promise you there are giant gnats that bite the hell out of you. They are the size of palm berries, leaving boils just as big." He shows him a circle. "As a kid, I would not listen to my father and get boils the size of your button on your uniform all over." Jeff points at Henry's buttons. "But hey it's up to you, do what you want."

Henry quickly sprays himself all over and says, "Any more helpful tips I should know?"

Jeff holds up some socks and replies, "You got

two pairs of these, right? Being this close to the Sun makes Rydean's surface a rainforest, besides the Red Waste. Which is a twelve-mile-long desert with red sand from which it gets its name. It is the rainy season which makes the ground a soggy mess." He shakes his head.

Luke walks by holding his gear and says, "Also, know everything out here wants to kill you," in a severe tone.

Henry's hands were shaking, but he was eager to prove himself. "I got you. Eyes on a swivel." He grabbed his pack and his blaster and walked down the ramp with the rest of the crew. As they leave the Dark Wolf, Henry asks, "Where is this rain you were talking about?" Looking around expecting a downpour.

Jeff is surprised and replies, "I don't know what is happening. It's normally coming down by this time of year."

Commander Gore comes running out of the Command Center and greets Captain Mitchell. "Hello, Captain, it's an honor to meet you, sir. What can I do for you?" He shakes his hand.

Jeff interrupts showing concern for his home. "What is going on here? It's normally pouring by now this time of the year."

Commander Gore looks at the sky and replies, "Yes, it's been like this for months. The plants are starting to suffer, and the ecosystem is starting to break down. Weather patterns are becoming erratic, and being this close to the sun is not helping. I hear you can see the black spots on it now. Did you see it on your way down?"

"No, we were in a hurry. We are on orders from the emperor. My crew and I are headed to Bearsekk to meet with a builder. We are going to need some speeders. Can we make it through?"

The Commander starts acting sketchy and replies, "I believe so. It's been a while since I've been there. We need to go to my office to get the keys."

"Is everything ok Commander?"

"Yes Captain, just a little under the weather." He fakes coughs.

"Ok, then I will leave three of my crew back with the ship. One is injured, and we are running low on supplies, so we will need some," Captain Mitchell replies.

As they walk into the inner wall door, he says, "We don't have much, but I got you, sir. Is there something I need to know about this builder from Bearsekk? I didn't get a report on him. "

"No, it's something the emperor sent us to deal

with," Cap replies, walking behind him to his office to grab the keys for the speeders. The speeders on Rydean are different due to the terrain and the narrow tunnels through the caves. They are bikes with two fans parallel to the ground for tires so that they can hover on the rough rainforest floor and easily maneuver through the tunnels.

As they walk to the motor pool, he becomes uneasy and says, "I hope everything is okay and you find who you are looking for."

They walk into the motor pool and load up into three of them and zoom out of the front gate.

The commander returns to his quarters, calls Shilyn, and says, "The infamous Captain Mitchell is headed your way. What should I do?"

She stands up and yells, slamming her dagger on

her desk, "What do I pay you for? How did you not know they were coming? Did he not give you a warning about this?" Her eyes glowed red in anger. She was once a hunter of a Newwart. After the rebellion, she left and became a Thug Lord. She has waist-length dreads that are black as night and skin white as snow. She is wearing a black Tricorn hat, black slacks, a black leather Victorian jacket with red desert Kast flower designs, and a white sword running through it.

He shakes in fear. "No, I wasn't warned they were coming here. They never come here. We are a little shit post."

She yells, "Something is going on, you imbecile!" as she slams her phone.

The Communications chief walks into the Dark Wolf's engine room, where Lily works on panels below deck to check that everything is good. She leans over and taps Lily and says, "Ma'am."

Lily jumps and says, "Holy smokes, you scared the heck out of me. What can I do for you, chief?"

"I didn't mean to scare you; I need to tell you something." Lily puts her tablet down, gets off the floor, and replies, "It's all good. What's up chief?"

She moves closer to her and whispers, "You and your friends are in grave danger."

Lily is surprised by this news. She grabs her blaster off one of the pipes and replies, "What the hell is going on, chief?"

The chief motions for her to be quiet and whispers, "A few months back, Shilyn, a Thug Lord in Bearsekk, started sending her men to the post once a month to get drilling supplies and weapons from Commander Gore. I think he was selling them to her."

Lily says, "My people are headed there! We have to warn them." They run to Dr. Beal's lab.

Millie, running behind her, says, "We can't. Commander Gore has taken over the comms room."

They hurry and rush into her lab, Lily says, "Dr. Beal, we have a problem."

Dr. Beal places the pen on her book, removes her glasses, stands up, and says, "Calm down, what's wrong, dear?"

She catches her breath and says, "The others are walking into a trap."

Dr. Beal, confused, replies, "What, how do you know this?"

The comms chief says, "Me, ma'am."

Walking over to them, Dr. Beal replies, "And who are

you?"

She snaps to attention and says, "Millie James, I'm the comms chief of the post." Her dark hair is in a bun that sticks out the back of her hat. She is very slender and has pale skin with freckles.

With a puzzled look, Dr. Beal says, "Are you related to Dorn James?"

Shocked that she knew her brother, Millie said, "Yes, he is my brother. I haven't seen him in a couple of days. How do you know him?"

Dr. Beal says, "We hear he is Rydeanin, you do not look Rydeanin."

Millie replies, "No, ma'am, I am Izealin like my parents. They adopted him before I was born and allowed him to learn his Rydeanin roots."

With a concerned look, Lily says, "That's who the team is meeting in Bearsekk."

In a panic, Millie replies, "What are we going to do? We only have each other left. I can't lose him?

Dr. Beal returns to her desk, grabs her tablet off the desk, pulls up the map of Morereck, and asks, "Millie, is there another way into the comms room?"

Millie points at a spot on the outer wall and says, "There are some tunnels under there that lead up under the comms room. We can get in that way and let them know what's happening.

Lily says, "Ok, I'll go with her, and you can watch over Roscoe."

Dr. Beal says, "OK, I will. Now, you guys, be careful and hurry. We only have an hour or so before they get there." They both head out of her lab toward the Dark Wolf's deck.

As the rest of the team enters the Lurnook rainforest, Captain Mitchell signals the sign to stop, and the team pulls over. The Lurnook rainforest is not as thick as other parts of Rydean's rainforest. It has light green vegetation and many flowers. It lies on the other side of the Opie River between Morereck and Bearsekk.

Razor approaches him and asks, "What is going on, Sir?"

Captain Mitchell replies, getting off his speeder and checking his map, "We are halfway there. We should do a radio check and grab some water from the river. This heat is no joke," wiping his head off. Oh, and go to the bathroom, Jeff. We heard you the whole way." They laugh at him, and Cap continues, "Ophelia, radio Dr. Beal, and Lily and let them know we are halfway there."

Ophelia picks up her radio and says, "Yes, sir. She tries to radio them, but there is no answer." She replies, "Cap, there is something wrong. I'm not getting through to them."

"We must split up Luke and Henry. You guys go back to base and see what's going on. The rest of us will continue to Bearsekk," Captain Mitchell says.

"Yes, sir," Luke and Henry jump on a speeder and rush back to Morereck.

Captain Mitchell and the others hop back on their speeder. Cap says, "Okay, let's go." They speed off toward Bearsekk.

They arrive at the entrance of the cave and head down the winding two-line tunnel to the gate of Berserk. The town is built into the caves like all cities and towns on Rydean due to the hot weather on the surface and the creatures that rule it, like the great Gin serpent, which grows to be 50 feet long and is known to swallow a man whole, as well as budsuns to worry about. They are green and yellow four-legged beasts whose razor-sharp claws and teeth can crush bones. The roofs of every house are built with red clay shingles for when it rains. The water can drain and run off easily. The walls of the houses are made from the rock around the caves and windomm from Ma'de. The cave's walls hold the water system of the cities, running pipes into every town and city, collecting the water from the ground above.

Captain Mitchell stops just before the meeting location. "They are supposed to meet us at the Den. We should try the others before we go as well."

Ophelia tries again, but she doesn't get an answer. "Cap, still no answer, sir."

"They should have made it by now," Cap says.

Ophelia has a bad feeling. "Should we turn back, sir?"

"They can handle whatever is happening there. Let's press on."

Luke and Henry reach Morereck, and Commander Gore yells, "Find the rest of Captain Mitchell's team now! A group of soldiers exits the second wall.

Henry and Luke duck into the forest foliage, hiding as the soldiers patrol.

Henry whispers to Luke, "What now?"

Luke looks around, thinking to himself, "Give me a minute. I'm thinking. OK, first, we must get to the Dark Wolf and see where the others are. Let's go!"

They began to move across the forest to the other side of Morereck, where the Dark Wolf is.

Following behind him, Henry says, "They seemed to have doubled the guards, so this will be harder than we thought."

"Yes, I see that," Luke replies. "Make sure you stay down and out of sight. We are almost there."

As they approach the Dark Wolf, they see Lily coming out of the outer wall with one of Morereck's soldiers behind her. Not knowing what is going on, they sneak up behind them and tackle the soldier to the ground.

Lily turns around and sees that it is Luke and Henry. She says, "What the hell, guys? Get off her." She slaps them up against their heads.

Confused by the situation, Henry gets up and

replies, "Ouch. What the hell is going on, Lily?"

Lily walks over, pushes Luke, grabs Millie's hand, and helps her. "She is helping us."

Luke says, "I'm sorry," getting up.

Millie, wiping herself off, says, "It's all good. I understand why you did what you did. I would have to for my friends."

Seeing a group of soldiers heading their way, they all kneel back down to avoid detection. Henry, very anxious, says again, "So what is going on? Are Roscoe and Dr. Beal, okay?"

Lily comforts him, placing her hand on his shoulder. She says, "They are fine. Dr. Beal had Randi put the ship on lockdown after we left, and she will only open it for us when we get the comms back up."

Luke is confused by the situation. "So, what happened?"

Millie looks at him and says, "The commander is working with the Thug Lord ShiLyn. When you guys left, he radioed her and told her you were coming. Then he shut down the comms room, ordering us all to leave and putting three different soldiers in the room that I didn't know."

Worried about the others, Henry says, "OK, what's the plan for getting the room back so we can warn them?"

Lily turns her arm over and clicks a button. A map holograph shows up. She points at the tunnels and says, "We planned to go in under them, get to the comms room, take it back over, and then radio you guys."

Luke replies, "Sounds like a solid plan. Now, with four of us, this should be easier."

Millie looks discharged and says, "My plan has only one flaw: We don't have explosives to blow a hole in the floor."

Henry has a big smile on his face and says, "Guys, I packed three of them." He shuffles through his bag and brings out three grenades. "I was hoping I would get to use them. Hell yeah!"

Millie kisses him on the cheek and says, "Thank you! You saved us." Henry turns red.

Luke shakes his head and says, "ok, then we have a plan. Lily and I will enter first and take down the first two guards. Millie, can you handle yourself?"

She snaps back at him and replies, "What's that mean? I was first in my class at the Cleat Academy regarding combat training and first in blaster shooting."

Luke is taken aback and impressed by her, saying, "I mean no disrespect. Then you come in after Lily and get the third guard. Henry, you cover our rear."

Henry says, "Got it. Can I at least activate the bombs?"

Lily answers worriedly as a group of soldiers pass by on the other side of the wall. "Yes, okay, we got the plan. Let's go before we get seen."

They head to the opening of the tunnels hidden behind some vines and crawl in.

As they crawl through the pipes to the comms room, Luke says, "So how did you know this was here?"

Millie replies, "I saw the original blueprint of the post once in the Commander's office."

Henry, amazed by her, says, "That is one hell of a memory."

She says, "Yeah, I have a photogenic memory. " As she hears the Commander above, she raises her fist and stops. "We are here."

They circle under the vent as Luke says, "OK, Henry, place the explosives. " He places one in the far corner, one in the middle, and one in the opposite corner of the vent and says, "OK, Get back."

They all back up as the explosives turn blue, and a loud boom goes off, tearing a hole into the floor of the comms room above. Luke and Lily head up through the hole in the ground first.

Not being able to see well because of the smoke, Luke orders, "Keep your eyes open and turn your blasters to stun. They are still one of us, just misguided."

They see the commander on the ground, knocked out.

Luke points at him, "Lily, check on him. We need him

alive if this plan is going to work."

"He is alive," she says, checking his vitals.

As Millie comes through, Luke says, "Good,

Millie. Get over there on the comms and contact

Captain Mitchell and the rest of the team before they get

to Bearsekk. Henry, tie up the others and cover the

door."

Henry ties the other soldiers up and runs over to

a table on the floor, flips it over, gets down behind it,

and points his blaster toward the door. "In position."

Luke looks back at Millie and says, "How are we

doing on the comms?"

"Working on the comms, Millie replies, "We have

a problem. He did something to kick me out."

Luke walks over to where she is sitting at the comms station and says, "How long will it take to fix it?"

Still trying to fix it, Millie says, "Give me about thirty minutes or so," as all the soldiers of Morereck start to gather outside the comms room to investigate the explosion.

Henry runs over and starts to barricade the door. He yells, "I don't think we have thirty minutes. You might want to make it 20."

Captain Mitchell and the rest of the team walk down the empty street of Bearsekk.

Razor, anxious and confused by the empty street, says, "Eyes up, I don't like this."

Jeff looked through the windows of the shops.

"Cap, where are all the people?"

Ophelia points at a building at the end of the corner and replies, "There it is, Sir."

Captain Mitchell walks up to the entrance of the Den, where the front door is locked. Seeing an arrow pointing down to a door at the end of the stairs, he tells his team, "This way."

Everyone heads down the stairs, and he opens the door to the bar, heading in first. He walks into a lightroom, the lights hanging down from a chain that goes all the way around the room, with a light hanging down every few feet. The room had black chairs, tables, and a large black bar with bar stools. You could see the bottles of alcohol behind the bartender on the edge of the cave wall sticking out.

Ophelia walks in behind him, looking around. No

one is there besides the bartender, so she says, "Sir, where are they? Jeff is right, sir. Where is everybody in this town?"

Captain Mitchell replies, "I don't know, but Jeff, go up there, ask her what is happening, and make it fast. We don't have time."

Jeff walks towards the bar while the rest of the team sits at a table near the entrance. He looks back and shrugs, smirking. "Come on, Cap. I'm nothing but professional."

ShiLyn walks into the Den with her two budsuns on a leash, and her four men follow behind.

They walk over to the table beside the team and sit down. ShiLyn yells at the bartender, "Five shots for my friends and me, and put it on my tab."

The bartender shakes in fear and says, "Yes,

Ma'am, right away," shaking while pouring the drinks.

Jeff leans over, grabs her hand, and comforts her. "Are you okay?"

ShiLyn picks her nails with her knife and replies, "Don't worry about her, my friend."

Still looking at the bartender, Jeff takes one of the shots, says, "I'm not your friend, but thanks for the shot," and drinks it.

ShiLyn replies, "I have not seen you before," as Jeff walks back to the group.

Captain Mitchell jumps in and replies, "Just waiting for an acquaintance of ours, that's all."

Shilyn turns her head to the side, examining Captain Mitchell up and down, snaps her fingers, and answers, "Wait, I heard a rumor that the Great Captain

Mitchell would be gracing us with his presence." She acts as if she didn't know he was coming.

Now on guard under the table, Captain Mitchell unlocks his holster and says, "We don't want any trouble. Like I said earlier, we are only here for our friends."

ShiLyn raises her leg to hold one of her men back and responds, "Captain, we are all civil here. If you give me your friend's name, maybe I can help?"

Jeff points to the bar and states, "We see your help. You have this poor woman scared. Why is that?"

ShiLyn holds her arms out and shrugs. "These people work for me, and I protect and feed them."

Jeff responds, "It seems to me that some people don't want it. They want their town back."

Razor presses her on the subject and replies, "What do you get for giving us what we want?"

She replies, "All I ask is for your builder after he has done what you need him for. Which is none of my business, Captain."

Curious by her request, Captain Mitchell says, "How do you know about him? And why do you need him?"

"I know many things, Captain, that's my specialty. Do we have a deal?" She holds her hand out.

Ophelia gets irritated by her and replies, "Enough of this charade. These people and this town are under the emperor's protection, and if you do not let them go now and tell us where our friend is, you will regret it."

ShiLyn laughs "Haha!" She stands up, walking towards the bar with her glass in her hand. "Girl, you and your team are all alone. I run this town, not the emperor, and if I wanted, my budsuns would eat you guys alive at the snap of my fingers, and no one would say a word." They growl at her.

Ophelia, now pissed off by her threat, pulls out her blaster and points it at ShiLyn. "You threaten a soldier of the imperial army. That's treason, and you are under arrest. Your oppression of this town and its people is over. Now, come with us!"

Laughing hysterically, she says to her, "You talk of oppression. Where were you while this so-called imperial army slaughtered my sisters on the Highyeah mountain?"

Razor looks her up and down and notices her ring. "You are from one of the mountain tribes."

"Yes, the last you all killed the others or made

them submit to your ways."

"Then just put your hands up and tell us what we want. No one needs to die." Ophelia says.

She looks at Ophelia closer. "You look like someone I once knew." She keeps walking to the bar.

Razor pulls his blaster out. "Stop moving and get on the ground."

She slowly walks back. "Girl, if your ancestors could see you, they would be ashamed. Protectors of the galaxy, my ass, come and make me." She reaches over the bar, grabs a blaster, and fires at them.

They return fire, and ShiLyn jumps over the bar and yells at her man, "Kill them all!" She fires at them, and her budsuns attack Jeff. Jeff is down on the ground as one of them is trying to eat him, and Ophelia shoots it in the side of the head with an exploding round, blowing it into pieces.

"Thanks," Jeff replies, wiping the blood off his face and crawling back to her.

Captain Mitchell and Razor flips over their table, facing it towards her men. The other budsun runs around the table and sinks its teeth into Razor's arm. He screams in agony, twirling the beats back and forth. He pulls out his digger and stabs it in the eye multiple times till it releases his arm.

Firing at the men, Cap glances over at Razor and sees he is hurt. "Razor, are you good?"

"I'm good." He pulls a wrap from his med kit and wraps his arm as blood pours out of his wound.

"No, my babies! Kill them all now! Shilyn goes crazy.

Ophelia and Jeff crouch behind another table, firing at the bar where Shilyn is.

Then, suddenly, the team starts taking fire from the entrance.

Jeff turns and starts firing at the door, yelling, "Cap, we are surrounded! This was a trap. Someone gave us up!" He keeps firing.

Ophelia looks around and replies, "Anyone see a way out?"

Razor firing at the other man looks at her, "No, just try and keep them back."

Shilyn laughs absurdly loud while shooting at them. "There is no way out. You are all going to die down here."

Then, suddenly, they hear blaster fire go off at the

top of the entrance, and two of ShiLyn's men come rolling down the stairs onto the bar floor dead.

The firing stops, and ShiLyn says, "Who the hell is up there?"

"Hey Cap, are you guys good? It's all clear up here," Henry replies.

"Heck yeah, Henry, we got you now," Jeff yells, pointing at Shilyn.

"Yes, Henry, we will be out in a minute," he responds, putting his blaster in his holster. He yells to ShiLyn, "You and your men have no way out now. We can do this one of two ways. Either you lay down your weapons and tell us what you did with our friends and the people of this town, or a squad of imperial soldiers will come down here and kill the rest of you and your men. It's your choice."

ShiLyn screams, slamming her blaster down on the bar, "Fuck! Drop your weapons, boys." Ophelia walks over and puts handcuffs on her. "Tight, don't you think?" she says to her.

Ophelia pulls her close and replies, "If you had done what we asked, you would not be going to the Istation. All you had to do was tell us where our friends are." She keeps her grip tight as they make their way up the stairs.

ShiLyn smirks. "You will never see them again."

Ophelia shoves her. "See now, that's why you're going to spend the next five years on ice on the Istation, collared."

ShiLyn smirks and whispers, "We will see."

Just as they reach the top of the steep stairs, Millie runs over and grabs Shilyn by the shoulders. She shakes her, screaming, "Where is my brother?" Millie punches

Shilyn and yells again, "Where is my brother?!"

Shilyn wipes the blood off her face with her

shoulder and says, "Nice hit, kid, but that's not going to

do it." Henry runs over and grabs Millie, restraining her

from hitting Shilyn again.

Captain Mitchell looks at Millie and yells, "Hey,

soldier, control yourself. Millie calms down, pulls herself

away from Henry, and walks off. Who is that, and what

happened at the post?"

Henry looks at Millie as she walks away and

answers, "This Newwartin and Commander Gore of

Morereck were working together for months, and they

didn't plan on anyone coming to the post. We just

happened to stumble upon their operation. The

commander called her soon as we left for Bearsekk, Sir."

Razor screams, "That traitor! They could have killed us!" He waves his fist in the air, momentarily forgetting about his wound. "Ah, shit."

"Are you good?" Cap asks as they all walk over to where the speeders and a squad of imperial soldiers are.

"I should be fine the fucker got me." He looks at the wound.

Ophelia throws ShiLyn to another soldier and says, "Collar her and put them in a transporter." She looks at Razor and says, "Father, are you okay?"

"I'm fine."

"Okay then. So, what happened to Luke and the others?" Cap replies.

Henry looks around the town, shakes his head, and says, "They are good now. We had to deal with the

Commander in the comms room. We were in a tight spot, but Millie got the comms to work just before his men could break down the door. We got him to tell the truth, and he is now being detained back at the post in a cell. None of us would be alive if it were not for her."

Captain Mitchell waves Millie back over and says, "What's your name, soldier?"

"Millie James, sir, Dorn James is my brother," she replies.

"I see now why you did what you did. Well, we are trying to find out where everyone is. You can stay with us if you can control yourself," Captain Mitchell responds.

"I'm sorry, sir, and I can, sir," she replies, snapping to attention.

"Well, then, let's talk to ShiLyn." They walked

over to her in the back of the speeder, where she was standing in a frozen state. They saw tears rolling down her face.

Millie stares at her, waves her hand in front of ShiLyn's face, and says, "I have never seen someone collared before."

Razor says, "Crazy, huh? It uses the same tech as the simulators on the drop ships, but it replays your worst fear repeatedly with no way out."

Millie replies, "That sounds dreadful."

Captain Mitchell pushes a button on his suit to deactivate the collar.

ShiLyn wakes and feels a blaster on the back of her head. Behind her, she hears a voice say, "So you want to tell us where our friends are now?" Jeff says.

ShiLyn pleads, "I'll do anything. Just don't put me back in there. They are in the Red waste at the dig site excavating the red diamond for Dust."

Millie angrily yells, "The Red Waste, are you kidding me? You deserve everything you get." She kicks the cage and hurries away, and the others follow her.

Henry replies, quickening his pace to stay caught up with her. "What's wrong, Millie? What's the Red waste?"

Millie shakes her head and answers, "The Red Moon is rising, and if wc don't hurry, everyone will die."

"Millie, wait." Henry was trying to catch her.

Ophelia, confused, replies, "Wait, what does a moon rising have to do with the people all being killed?"

With this horrifying look, Millie replies, "The Gin!

We must go now!"

Jeff replies, "That is some fairy tale the old Rydeanains once used to say, nothing more."

ShiLyn laughs and says, "We shall see. Tik Tok tik Tok."

Ophelia slaps the cage and yells, "Shut up, or I will collar you again." ShiLyn cowardly retreats to the other side of the cage and becomes quiet.

Captain Mitchell does not honestly believe her story. He replies, "We have to go get her brother either way, and we should also prepare for anything. Hey, soldier," he gestures to one of the imperial soldiers.

The soldier runs up to him and answers, "Yes, sir."

Captain Mitchell orders, "Take her back to the

post and lock her up next to Commander Gore. We will deal with them when we get back. Guys, grab your gear, and let's roll out!"

Henry jumps on a speeder and waves over to Millie. She runs over to his speeder and looks concerned, and he replies, "We will make it, I promise."

They all hop on the speeders and speed off through the empty town, down the tunnels, and into the forest, stopping just at the edge of the Lurnook rainforest. They arrived at the entrance of the Red Waste just as the Red Moon started to rise.

They hop off the speeders and take cover, seeing Shilyn's men, but they cannot see them.

Looking over to Captain Mitchell, Millie whispers, "We must hurry. What's the plan, Sir?'

Captain Mitchell points at Jeff and then up and

says, "Let me know what you see."

Jeff gets up, heads for a tree, and responds, "Yes, sir."

Jeff climbs the tree, "Man, I am getting too old for this." Getting to the highest branch, he stops, looks out, and sees the whole dig site through his scope. Hey Cap, you copy?"

"Yeah, Jeff, what are we looking at?" Cap responds.

"I got seven armed men, two on the back side of the dig site, three watching over the people while they dig standing with their backs to you, and two on the front entrance. I believe I can take out the front two before the others realize." while he is screwing in another barrel to his rifle.

"Razor, you and Ophelia come in from the East,

and they won't know what hit them."

"Father, are you sure you are good? I can easily handle them."

"I'm fine. Stop asking me that's an order."

Ophelia shakes her head. "Stubborn old man, fine." She pulls her blaster out.

"Henry, Millie, and I will hit the front. Let me know when you guys are in position."

"Yes sir," Razor and Ophelia replied.

Razor bends down behind a tree and calls Cap on the radio, "Cap, we are in position."

"Ok, here's the plan: we hit them first and swiftly on your mark, Jeff." Captain Mitchell orders.

Jeff takes aim and fires. Hitting both guards, he

says, "Now Cap!" The others charge the site, shooting all the guards that were watching over the people.

Razor and Ophelia start firing at the other two on the back end, but they retreat further into the Red Waste, so they do not pursue them.

Millie runs up to Dorn, hugs him before she leans back, punches him in the face, and yells, "Where the hell have you been?"

Dorn rubs his jaw and replies, "Dang, Millie, we lost track of time at a bar just outside of Toless. The music, drink, and vibes were too good to leave. You know how I get after a few."

Tekey-Espy laughs, "It was a hell of a time, though." They round up all the people and begin to leave.

Razor mutters, "You damn Rydeanins and you're

partying and killing," as he waves the people along,

"Come on, let's hurry people."

They feel the ground rumble, and Millie looks at

Dorn with a petrified look and screams, "The Gin,

RUN!" Everyone starts to scatter in all directions

Millie waves her hands towards the tree line and

yells, "No, no head for the tree line. It can't enter the

rainforest."

The Gin bursts out of the sand, covering up the

moon. It was so big, the red-scaled, green-eyed snake

with straight black pupils and fangs the size of a

Newwart woman. It looks down at all the townspeople

with all the red Dust all over them. It licks its mouth and

crashes down on a group, swelling the group whole and

submerging itself back into the sand.

Stunned by this, Jeff yells, "Run now, faster guys,

it's coming back," as he shoots at it.

They are all running when Dorn rolls his ankle and falls. Millie and Henry turn back to get him. Millie yells, "Come on, get up; it's coming. Can you run?" She grabs his hand and lifts him, trying to help, but Dorn's ankle is too messed up.

Henry points at a tower nearby and says," Let's get there," just as the rest of the team and the townspeople reach the tree line.

Captain Mitchell looks around and says, "Where are Henry, Dorn, and Millie?"

Tekey-Espy, bent over, huffing and puffing, replies, "I thought they were behind me."

Captain Mitchell radios Jeff and says, "Jeff, do you have eyes on Henry and them?

"Yes, Sir, they are about ten yards out, Cap," he responds.

"Henry, are you guys, ok?" Cap radios him.

Henry wraps Dorn's ankle and replies, "Dorn has a bum ankle, Sir."

"Can he move? Cap responds.

Henry looks up at Dorn, and he nods his head, and Henry replies, "He can move, Sir."

"Ok. Jeff, do they have an opening?" Cap says.

Jeff looks down the scoop of his blaster and says, "Cap, they've got a ten-second opening coming up."

"Henry, did you read that? In ten seconds, I want you guys to jump and run like hell," Cap tells him.

"Roger that Cap," Henry responds. He looks over

at Millie and Dorn. "We have a window we need to jump and hall ass here in ten seconds. Are we good?" Dorn tries to get up and put pressure on it and falls. Sir, we have a problem."

Cap looks towards the tower and replies, "What is it?"

He states, "Dorn can't put any pressure on his ankle. We need another plan."

Jeff yells, "Cap, there is no time, they need to go now!"

Henry looks around, thinking about what to do, and says, "Millie, get him up now!" They get to the tower's edge, and Henry stands behind them and says, "Run!" as he pushes them off the side.

Millie and Dorn hit the ground, and she helps him to his feet as they start running towards the rainforest. Henry distracts the Gin by firing at it from the other side of the tower.

Millie, running with a limping Dorn, yells, "What the hell, Henry! Get out of there now!"

Henry, trying not to sound scared, replies, "Just get your brother to safety, "as The Gin bursts out of the sand and stares at him.

When Millie and Dorn reach the tree line, she looks back, sees this, and yells, "Henry, no!"

Henry drops his blaster and pulls out two swords. He turns the handles, and the swords become engulfed with an orange laser. He closes his eyes and says to himself, "Roscoe, I'm sorry, my friend. May we meet in the stars." He runs, yelling, and jumps at the serpent just as it is coming down to strike the tower. He stabs it just above its left eye and slices down the left side of the serpent's face. The Gin freaks out in pain and throws

Henry across the sand as The Gin submerges into the sand again and retreats in the other direction.

Millie runs towards Henry, fearing the worst. She gets to him and sees that he is not breathing. She starts CPR on him and says, "Don't you die on me, you fool!" He coughs and begins to breathe again. She hugs him and then punches him in the chest. "You idiot. Why did you do that?"

"Someone had to," he replies, coughing and then winces immediately afterward.

She comforts him then kisses him and says, "Thank you."

When the rest of the team arrives, she helps him reach his feet. He replies, "You're welcome."

Cap and Razor walk up to him as he dusts himself off, and Cap says, "You all good?"

"Yes, sir all good."

Jeff excitedly runs over to Henry, impressed by his courage and what he did, and yells, "Dang wild man, didn't know you had that in you. I see you, young fella. I see you." At the same time, the rest of the team walks up to him.

Ophelia slaps him and says, "If you need a recommendation for Cleat Academy, I've got you."

Henry smiles and replies, "Thanks, guys."

Jeff looks down at one of the knocked-over barrels and sees bags of Dust, and yells for the team to come over, "Guys, look at this, the fuckers."

They walk over to him and see eight barrels full of Dust, and Ophelia shakes her head and says, "They are just exploiting these people for money, those cowards."

"Cap, what do you want us to do with this?" Razor asks.

"Burn it and make it fast. We must go," Cap orders.

"Luke was right. Are we going to be worth saving in the end?" Ophelia says as they get the Dust all in a pile to burn.

Walking ahead of them, Razor says, "Alright, alright, let's go. We must get back to Morereck and get these people home. You heard the captain get a move on."

"Yes, sir," they say while the others load the people onto the speeder transporters and prepare to return to Bearsekk.

Captain Mitchell says, "Light it up, and let's roll."

"Roger that, sir, Ophelia replies as she sets the pile on fire, and they drive off to Bearsekk.

Captain Mitchell and the team arrive back at Bearsekk, and the people are overjoyed. He tells a squad of imperial soldiers to ensure everything is safe and the people of Bearsekk are protected. They load up ShiLyn and her men and head out to Morereck. They arrive at the front gate of Morereck, where Dr. Beal and Luke are waiting for them.

As he pulls up to the gate, Captain Mitchell says, "It's been a hell of a week. " He and the team get off their speeders and unload the prisoners.

Dr. Beal, following alongside him and the rest of the team with their gear in their hands, replies, "I know." She nods at ShiLyn and her men. "Who are they?

Looking back at ShiLyn as she moves to the

holding cells, Cap replies. "She is the one who was working with the Commander, and you wouldn't believe this: They were mining the Red Diamond for Dust."

"Wow, what is going on?"

"I don't know but a lot is happening here, and I believe we are just scratching the surface."

"At least we got the builder, right?" as she looked at Dorn and Millie holding each other.

Captain Mitchell chuckles and says, "Yeah, and it came with a hell of a story about that one." Looking at Henry. How is Roscoe?"

Dr. Beal lowers her head and shakes. "Same."

Captain Mitchell sighs and replies, "Let's get to work then. We will need it done when he wakes."

"Yes let's," she replies, and they enter the second

gate of Morereck.

Ophelia sees them taking ShiLyn to the brig and follows. She steps in front of her cell and unmutes it. "You said earlier I looked like someone you knew. Did you know my parents?"

ShiLyn gets up and approaches her. "Yes, your mother and I grew up together. She was a great mountain woman. You look like her."

"I do." Ophelia steps closer. "What was she like?"

"She was fearless, but your father was her downfall. She moved into the city, and it got her killed."

Ophelia becomes enraged. "You people killed her because she didn't want to live your way anymore?"

"You would believe that story they spent. It was the very people you serve who did that." ShiLyn turns her back to her.

"No, that is not how that happened," Ophelia yells.

She turns around, heated. "What do you know? I was there! They came into our village and killed everyone because of your parents."

"Shut up!"

Shilyn smirks. "Just like your parents, weak."

"You know nothing." Ophelia mutes her cell and leaves.

Razor watches her leave, walks into the brig behind her, and unmutes ShiLyn's cell. "What did you say to my daughter?"

"Only the truth." She laughs

"You stay away from her with all your lies."

"It doesn't matter. You are all murderers and will die soon for what you have done." She laughs hysterically.

"You are crazy." He mutes it and walks out.

ShiLyn curls up in a bowl and continues to laugh.

Chapter 9

Back on Izeal, as the summit gets on its way, the Chancellors walk down to the Chancellor's Dome, a beautiful glass dome structure with marble stone statues of the previous Emperors outside of it, surrounding the circle structure. Inside is a circle theater with a chair in the middle where the emperor sits. The Chancellor's seats are marble stone slabs with silk pillows on them and the flags of their planets behind them.

They enter, Chancellor Riley looks around, walks over to Chancellor Graves and Cantrell, and says, "Where is Andrea?"

They look at each other, confused by her action. Chancellor Graves replies, "We have no idea. We all agreed to talk to her here."

Chancellor Cantrell dismisses her absence. "You

know how the Lanardins are. They need to pray just to move," he snickers.

Chancellor Graves chuckles and says, "Or she has had too much wine."

With a puzzled look, she replies, "Still, I feel something is wrong." They enter the Dome lobby.

Chancellor Graves sees her distraught and replies, "I'm sure she is fine, but if you feel this way, send an envoy after her."

"I will after this," She responds.

The dong goes off, and they all start to make their way to their seats, noticing that the emperor has yet to show up.

Chancellor Gann quickly stands up and states, "We should vote on order 23 right now before he arrives."

Chancellor Rinehart stands and replies, "Should we not at least hear him out?"

He gets angry and yells, "He has had years to fix the problem, and all he has done is keep secrets from us. My people say he has Captain Mitchell and his team running around on secret missions, doing who knows what, and we know nothing about it."

Chancellor Riley shows compassion for him and replies, "We know what you have lost, Drake, but we have to do this right."

He slams his fist down on the arm of his chair and replies, "They were children, Jocelyn. A tear rolls down his eye. This is personal. We must do this for all of us and the children to come. We have lost too much."

While they start arguing over whether to vote on

it, Margo, disguised as one of the guards, overhears, sneaks out of the room, and calls Kelly. "The Chancellor's plan to execute order 23. You must do something now if you are, and I want my money put into my account now. I have something I need to do. My sister is not here."

Kelly looks at her guard. "It's happening. Get my ship ready, just in case. Margo, your money will be in your account. It was nice doing business with you. Tell your sister I will speak with her soon."

Margo hops on her ship. "You as well, Empress and I will." She throws her earpiece away, and her ship zooms off.

Emperor Noah is in the throne room waiting on news from Captain Mitchell. He's hoping to give good news to the Chancellors, that it would be enough to please them and the people, shutting down a rebellion.

Just as Captain Mitchell's message arrives, Kelly storms into the throne room and yells "Father, the Chancellors are voting on order 23 to overthrow you. I told you, Father! I knew those fucking traitors would do this!"

He walks over to his throne and holds up a pad. "It's okay. I just received good news from Captain Mitchell, which should make them happy and save us all."

She walks up to him, grabs the pad from his hand, and throws it across the room, breaking it. "Why are you trying to appease these traitors, Father? They conspired against us. All our enemies are in one place." She points at The Chancellor's Dome. "Let's strike now and wipe them from the face of the galaxy!"

He becomes saddened and ashamed. "My dear, you have not been the same since you lost your child, and maybe that was my failure as a father. I was not there for you when you needed me like your mother would have been. It made you cruel and cold. You feel nothing but hate. You only desire power and blood and I cannot let you ascend to the throne."

Kelly is hurt and angered by her father's words. "You cowardly and weak old man. You will no longer rule me and my countrymen." She pulls her blade out from her back and stabs him in the heart.

He falls back onto his throne, blood spewing everywhere, and he utters, "Matthias."

Kelly bends down next to her father's throne, holds his head up, and smirks. "Do you want to know a secret, Father?" She leans in and whispers. "You took everything from me not just a son but what was mine. So I killed your precious Matthias, not Rachel. A son for a son. I started the conflict between you and the

Chancellors."

He coughs up blood and says, "Why, my dear, he was your brother?"

She looked at him and replied, "My half-brother. That bastard Ma'dein would have given it all up for her—my throne, my birthright. I was the firstborn, and he wanted to give what was mine to the people."

He smiles. "I hope you find peace one day, my dear," he utters with his last breath.

A tear rolls down her cheek, and she wipes it away and whispers in his ear, "Goodbye, Father, may we meet in the stars."

Just as she places his head down, the emperor's guards enter to get him for the summit and see her over his body, blood running down from him. They start to fire at her, screaming, "Murderer! The emperor is dead!

She killed him!"

Diving behind the throne, she returns blaster fire, screams. "Come get some!"

The hidden door behind the throne opens, and it's her guard. "Come with me now, " he fires at the guards. I figured you could use some help, so let's go." She ducks out the door just as Chancellor Gann enters the throne room and waves at him. They shut the door.

Chancellor Gann and the guards run to the wall, but there is no way in. "Find her now!" They search everywhere as she quickly escapes to her ship, leaving the city.

Chapter 10

Rachel is on her drop-ship about to pass Tearocon when she falls asleep and wakes in the Dream realm. Hearing The Dream King calling her, she makes her way to the castle. Walking down the throne room hall, the Knights roar and bite at her.

She approaches the throne, and he roars, "Where is the boy, Rachel?

She falls to her knees and pleads with him, "I'm sorry, my King, he is dead. I didn't mean for it to happen."

"Lies." He roars. "Why would you lie to me?"

She pleads, "Uncle-"

Tsk, he interrupts her shaking his head and waving his finger. "You have tried everything to keep him from me, but you will bring him right to me. I see everything." He snaps his fingers, and his Knights appear, surrounding her. He turns his back and says, "You have failed me for the last time. Get her."

She stands up, dreams up a double pole-blade, and yells, "You will be stuck here forever."

He drops his hand, and they start to attack her, overpowering her. They begin to tear her apart and beat her nearly to death. Just before she passes out, she utters "Roscoe."

Roscoe then wakes suddenly and says, "Mother."

Roscoe blinks and looks around the room as his tube slides open and alarms go off. Lily hears them and investigates the medical bay, seeing Roscoe's tube slide open.

She yells, "Guys," as she runs in and hugs him.

"Don't you ever do that to me again? I don't know what I would have done without you. I love you, Roscoe."

Roscoe hugs her back, his head still a little cloudy from the coma, and replies, "I love you too, and I'm so sorry I should have said something sooner about the dream weaving."

"Don't worry about that now," she says, holding back tears.

Everyone else starts to pour into the room to check on him.

Henry hugs him, "I'll never leave your side again, little buddy. I'm sorry."

"I'm sorry, too. No hard feelings brother," he says.

Dr. Beal comes in with a big smile on her face,

"Thanks be to the Creator! You are alive! I owe you an apology. I should have told you who she was initially, and I'm so sorry for that."

Roscoe replies "I forgive you." They hug as everyone surrounds his tube.

"I forgive all of you and I'm sorry I ran off like that. I promise never again."

They all hug before Lily helps him out of his tube.

With her help, Roscoe walks over, sits in a chair, and asks, "How is the portal coming along?"

"Babe, you don't need to worry about that. You just got up, Roscoe."

Looking up at her, he puts his hand on hers and replies, "While I was out, I think I heard my mother in the Dream realm calling me. She needs my help."

Lily pulls her hand from him and says, "So what! How do you know it's not The Dream King planning a trap for you?"

He grabs her hand and says, "Lily, I know what she has done, but she is my mother, and I believe she is hurt."

Lily sighs, understanding, and replies, "I still don't like her, but I'll go for you."

Roscoe leans, kisses her hand, and says, "Thank you, Lily. So where are we, Cap?"

Cap stands up and says, "Follow me." They all head out of the Dark Wolf and to the basement underneath Morereck. Just as they reach the top of the stairs, they can see the bright lights sparking off the portal, a large circular gateway.

Cap yells, "Hey, Dorn, are you almost done?" He

does not hear him, so Cap yells again, "Hey, Dorn, are you ready?" Dorn still does not listen to him, so Razor walks up and kicks Dorn's leg.

Dorn pulls down his mask, removes his earbuds, and replies, "What's up, guys?"

Cap helps him up and replies, "All good, so where are we with the portal?"

Dorn examines the portal and says, "Give me one more day. I just need to weld a couple more pieces, and then we should be ready. I will just need the power core."

Cap looks at the portal, turns around, looks at his team, and says, "You hear him. Get ready. Tomorrow, we end this and save our people."

They all cheer and head out, but Roscoe looks at the portal, thinking about his mom.

Lily walks up behind him and says, "Are you okay?"

Roscoe looks back at her and says, "Yes, I was thinking about her and if we will be there in time." He looks back at the portal.

Still worried about him, Lily hesitantly says, "We will, and she will be okay." She places her hand on him and says, "I'll see you on the ship." She walks past Henry as he and Millie approach Roscoe, puts her hand on his arm, and says, "He needs you."

Henry puts his hand on hers and says, "He will be ok. He is stronger than we think, but I got him."

She replies, "Thank you, Okay, I'll see you shortly." Then she leaves for the Dark Wolf to get her gear.

Henry and Millie walk up to Roscoe, and Henry

says, "Is that not amazing?"

Roscoe replies, "Yes, it is," as they look at the portal. "I also see a lot has changed since I was out," he says, looking at Millie and Henry holding hands.

Henry completely spaced, forgetting she was there, and replied, "Oh, sorry. This is Millie, my, uh?"

Roscoe laughs. "Ha, hi. It's Roscoe. Nice to meet you. " He reaches out his hand to shake hers.

Millie reaches out her hand and says, "Nice to meet you. I've heard a lot about you. I'm glad you're okay."

"Thanks." He replies, looking back at the portal.

Henry says, "We got this. Don't worry. Let's go get some training."

Roscoe nods and replies, "Let's go." They head

back to Dark Wolf to grab their gear.

He gets to his room and puts on his gear. He looks at himself in the mirror, sighs, and says, "I will save you, mother."

He hears a knock at the door, and the voice on the other side says, "Hey, it's me.

When he opens the door, it's Lily. She can tell how sore he is and replies, "You can give it another day, Roscoe. You just woke up."

"No, I'll be fine. My mother needs me, I need to work on my powers. I don't know how long she has left, and I must be ready.

She pulls the string on his uniform, tightening it up. "Ok."

Roscoe walks to the training room where Henry is

already waiting for him. "Hey, man, are you ready?"

"Yes, let's link up." They walk over to the

helmets, and they put them on.

They show up in a dojo, both in a Gi. "So, what

do you want to work on first?" Henry asks.

"I have learned it happens when I get emotional

and anxious."

"Ok, then put your hand up and defend yourself."

Henry charges to fight him.

He and Henry start throwing punches, blocking

each other's attacks. Then Henry catches Roscoe in the

jaw. Roscoe's eyes glow blue, and Shadow jumps behind

him and kicks him in the back, knocking Henry across

the room.

Roscoe awakens and realizes what he did. He runs

over to check on Henry. "Shoot, man. I am sorry." He helps him up.

Henry wipes himself off. "It's all good but I don't think I can take another of those kicks. What else can you do?"

"When my mom and I were in the void she could multiply herself."

Henry excitedly says, "Try that."

"Okay." Roscoe nods, closes his eyes, and tries, but nothing happens.

"Nothing is happening, you've got to concentrate," Henry says, waiting and watching.

"I am, be quiet. Dang." Roscoe closes his eyes, chuckling.

Henry laughs "Ok, ok."

Roscoe kneels, concentrates harder, and then begins to multiply all around Henry, but it does not last long.

"Shoot, you did it!" Henry says all excited.

"Yeah, but it didn't last," Roscoe says disappointed. "It's ok man. You just woke up. Let's call it a day. You need to get some rest." Henry helps him to his feet.

"Yeah, you're right." They take off their helmets.

Roscoe goes to leave, but Henry stops him. "Hey, brother?"

Roscoe turns around. "Yeah, man?"

"We will save her together; promise you're not in this alone. I love you, man."

"Thanks, brother. I know." Roscoe turns, holding

his fist up, and walks out. Henry places his helmet back on, continuing his training.

Lily and Roscoe approach the rest of the team the following day at the portal's entrance. Just as Captain Mitchell made his way up to the front of the portal, he said, "So this is the plan. Team A will be Roscoe, Henry, Luke, and me. We will find The Dream King and kill him. Team B is Razor, Lily, Ophelia, and Jeff. You all will find the missing people. After we get them back safely, we can collect the Pearium. The rest of you will guard the portal; if we fail, you must blow the portal and not let anything or anyone through."

They all look around at each other, feeling the gravity of the situation, and say "Yes, sir."

Dr. Beal walks up to the panel, inserts the core, and turns it to the right, powering on the portal. Purple lightning strikes as they see the Dream Realm.

"Ok, let's go, " Captain Mitchell says, entering first.

They all follow behind him, but just as Henry is about to enter, Millie says, "Hey, don't worry. I'll be right here when you get back."

Henry looks back at them, blows her a kiss, and enters. Henry comes through, looks around, feels absolute fear curl up his spine, and says, "Oh my, I do not like this place." Shaking his head.

"Ok, turn on your life monitor and cameras so they can monitor us on the other side," Captain Michell says. As they each turn their equipment, purple lightning strikes, and they can see The Dream King's castle in the distance.

Roscoe looks at Lily and says, "Hey, I need you to promise me something."

Lily turns on her camera and answers, "Yes, dear, what is it?"

Roscoe grabs her hand and replies, "If I don't make it, please make sure my mom does. I know she has done some evil things and will have to pay for it, but she is my mom. Don't kill her, please."

Lily pauses briefly and says, "You will make it."

Roscoe says, "Lil, promise me."

Lily shakes her head, "I promise."

The team starts to make their way to the castle, walking through the purple smoke that covers the Dream Realm's floor. As they reach the stone door of the castle and enter, Cap says, "Here we go. You guys know what to do; keep your eyes peeled."

They hear a blood-curdling voice that says, "You

have made a grave error coming here, boy. The voice seemed like it surrounded them.

Roscoe says, "There went our element of surprise."

Captain Mitchell, walking towards the door to the throne room, replies, "It's okay. We're sticking with the plan."

Razor waves to his team and says, "You heard the Cap. Let's head down this way and find the people."

Lily and Luke hug, and Luke says, "Find mom ok."

Holding her brother, Lily replies, "I will. Do me a favor and keep an eye on him. I love you both," and she walks away.

Luke watches his sister walk away as he whispers,

"I will, and I love you. May we meet in the stars," and runs to catch up to the others.

Razor and his team headed down a winding staircase with purple fire torches every few feet. They reached the dungeon and saw hundreds of people looking up at the purple haze in a trance.

Jeff stands before one of the people, waving his hand in their faces, but gets no response. He says, "Hey, Razor, have you ever seen anything like this before?"

Confused by what he sees, Razor replies, "No, I don't know what this is."

Walking down a few rows from the others, Lily finds her mother and yells, "Mom, wake up. Guys over here, I found her."

The rest of them run over to where she is. Lily says, "What is wrong with her?"

"We don't know. We tried to get the people to wake, but nothing worked," Ophelia says.

Lily wraps her arms around her mom and says, "We can't just leave them here."

Ophelia, feeling helpless, responds, "We won't."

They hear a cough and a weak voice in the distance say, "You can't."

Flashing a light to the right of them, just ahead, there are some cells. They walk up to them and find Rachel lying there with her head up against the cell, her body covered in cuts and bruises.

Ophelia bends down by her and says, "What did you say?"

Rachel Coughs again and answers, "You can't move them. What are you doing here?"

Lily steps closer to her cell. "Your son. You know, the one you left for dead. He is here to save you, so you need to give us something more than we can't."

She starts to freak out. "No, no, you don't understand. I shot Roscoe on purpose."

"Wait, what, why? I have been with some crazies, lady, but you take the cake. He is your son." Jeff responds.

She grabs the bar, pulls herself up with all her strength, and says, "I know. You don't know what that did to me, but I had to do it."

Lily, confused, yells, "What would make you think this?"

She looks at Lily and says, "Come here, I will tell you."

Lily leans closer to the cell, and Rachel whispers, "When your child is born, you will do anything to protect them." Rachel looks back at the others as Lily thinks about what she said. "The Dream King has wanted him since he took that drink that awoke the powers inside him."

Lily steps back and replies, "What do you mean he wants him?"

"He wants him as his vessel into our world, and if that happens, he'll roll over everyone and everything. We must get him out of here," she states, coughing between breaths.

Razor walks up to the cell, pulls out his lock pick, unlocks it, holds her up, and says, "Explain."

Finding it hard to breathe, she says, "He needs to merge with him. He is the last male in our line, so he's the only way back. Ever since he was born, I have been doing what I could to keep Roscoe off his radar by doing everything he wanted."

Jeff says, "So what changed? Your people came for him on Izeal?"

She lowers her head and says, "He drank beer. That and the pills mixed with his blood woke up his power. Like I said, The Dream King felt him as soon as his powers awoke. He sent us after him. I tried multiple times to get him to run at the market on San-Van. Where is Roscoe now?"

Lily, starting to understand, replies, "He is with the rest of the team going after The Dream King."

Rachel yells, "No, we have to go help them! He is not ready; we must go!"

Ophelia looks at Razor and says, "What about

these people?"

She replies, "They will wake when we kill him."

Razor looks at them and says, "We have to trust that she is right. We must kill him first, then save the people." They head back to the stairs when a knight appears in front of them.

Razor pulls out his katana and says, "I got this." He runs at the knight, slides under its legs, and stabs it in the back. The knight roars and disappears into a cloud of smoke. They hear growls, and multiple purple eyes appear in the dark.

Rachel yells, "There are too many, and we must go now! They run up the stairs shooting the knights as they pursue them.

Roscoe looks around the vast throne room and hears a sinister voice say, "Foolish boy, you shouldn't have come here. Finally, I can leave this place."

Captain Mitchell pulls his blaster out and says, "Get ready." Everyone pulls out their weapons as the room fills with purple smoke.

With his arms spread wide, Roscoe yells, "You want me? Come and get me; show yourself!" The Dream King appeared out of the purple smoke before his throne.

He slowly walks down his steps. Some of his knights appear around him. "Here I am, boy. You should be careful what you wish for. Kill them all, but the boy is mine."

His knights charge the team. Purple smoke and orange-blaster fire consume the room, causing them to split up.

Luke says, "Anyone have eyes on Roscoe?" as he

slices one of the knights down.

Henry sees Roscoe walking towards The Dream King and yells, "No, Roscoe!" As more knights bum-rush him, he fights them back with his sledgehammer.

Roscoe walks towards The Dream King. "This is between you and me. Leave my friends alone." He closes his eyes, and a blue-flamed katana appears in his hand. He opens his eyes, glowing blue, and says, "I am going to end you," running toward him.

The Dream King conjures up a purple scythe and charges at him, "You will be mine."

Roscoe shadow jumps to him and they begin to fight. They swing and block each other's attacks. The Dream King kicks Roscoe down, and he spins on his knees, pulls out his blaster, and fires multiple shots at The Dream King's face. Purple smoke bellows from his body, making Roscoe think he hit him.

The Dream King pops out of the smoke and says, "My turn." A big multi-barrel blaster appears in his hand, and he fires at him.

Roscoe bends down to brace the attack, and a purple shield surrounds him. With the last ounce of her power, Rachel places it around him.

The Dream King in rage throws his scythe, stabbing her in the gut.

She drops to the ground, and Lily runs over by her side, holding her head up. "I got you, Rachel."

As she is dying, she reaches over, puts her hand on Lily's belly, and says, "I hope you are a better mother to yours than I was to mine." Then, Rachel takes her final breath.

Lily closes her eyes, "May we meet in the stars," folding her arms.

The shield around Roscoe falls. He falls to his knees and screams in pain, "Mom!"

While the rest of the team fights around him, they become overrun. Roscoe becomes overcome with anger, as he looks around, seeing his new family in danger, he screams, "You are going to die for that!"

He charges up, and Shadow jumps in front of The Dream King with a club he manifests in his hand, knocking him into the air. Roscoe does it again, appearing behind him and knocking The Dream King down to the ground, causing a caravan on the floor. He dreams up an energy ball and fires it at The Dream King. Blue smoke pours out of the hole. Roscoe stops to check if he is dead.

The Dream King wipes blood off his face and exits the smoke. "That's all you got? Let me show you real power."

The roof starts to creak and break apart. Using his power, he grabs parts of the castle's roof as he rises. Laughing, he aims them at everyone. Raining pieces down upon them as purple lightning strikes all over.

Roscoe yells, "No!" He shadow jumps in front of The Dream King, breaking his hold on the flying stones, and tackles him outside the castle towards the cliff's edge. Roscoe and The Dream King pull their weapons out and shadow jump toward each other once more. Their weapons clash as the lightning strikes in the distance.

Henry sees them fly out of the roof. He shoots a knight in the face, smashes another in the head, and exits the castle. He races to follow them and protect Roscoe.

Henry gets outside the castle, looking for them, but can barely see anything because it's pitch black, and they are moving so fast. All he can see are their weapons clashing in the sky.

The Dream King kicks Roscoe to the ground. He comes crashing down, shaking the ground like an earthquake. He dreams up his blue katana as The Dream King attacks him, swinging his scythe at him. Roscoe blocks The Dream King's attack as he holds all his weight down upon Roscoe. They are in a standoff, and no one gives way to the other. The Dream King kicks Roscoe to his knees and multiplies surrounding him. They all attack Roscoe, punching and kicking him. They stop, and The Dream King laughs as he conjures up an energy ball, and they all fire simultaneously. Boom, boom, boom, the blast knocks Henry back.

Roscoe's bruised and battered body lay there, not moving. The Dream King pulls the purple smoke around them, forcing it to hold Roscoe down. "I will kill everyone you love with your own body." He plunges his hand into his chest, and the merge begins.

Roscoe screams in pain. "Ahhhh!"

"You are mine," The Dream King laughs.

Henry sees this. "No! Roscoe!" He picks up a blaster and fires two shots, hitting The Dream King in the shoulder. He runs over tackling the Dream King. Henry and the Dream King fall over the edge, into the Pearium.

The Dream King's Knights disappear, and Lily looks around for Roscoe, screaming his name, not knowing what has happened. They hear screams, and Lily and the team run out of the castle to investigate, only to see Roscoe in agony at the cliff's edge. "Henry!"

Lily runs up to Roscoe. "What happened?"

"He is gone. Oh, my Creator, Henry is gone!"

Roscoe cries out.

Epilogue

The Dream King awakes in a new realm covered in darkness. "Where am I?"

A voice in the Dark laughs and replies, "You thought you could take it from me. I gave you your power; you were supposed to give me the vessel in exchange. Now, you will die for your betrayal!"

The Dream King becomes afraid and yells, "No, no!"

You can hear a slice through the air, and The Dream King's body splits in half and falls to the ground. The voice says, "One down, one more to go, then I'm coming for you, Father." As a deep and sinister laugh echoes.

Author Notes

Jamel P. Bates is the author of his debut sci-fi fantasy novel. Renowned for his creativity and vivid imagination, he crafts captivating worlds that draw readers in. Jamel resides in Northeastern Oklahoma with his girlfriend, five sons, and two dogs. In his downtime, he enjoys watching Oklahoma State University dominate on the field and immersing himself in the world of Game of Thrones.